P9-DFL-171

BOOKS BY CARLOS FUENTES

Aura

Distant Relations

Constancia and Other Stories for Virgins

Terra Nostra

The Campaign

The Old Gringo

Where the Air Is Clear

The Death of Artemio Cruz

The Good Conscience

Burnt Water

The Hydra Head

A Change of Skin

Christopher Unborn

Diana: The Goddess Who Hunts Alone

The Orange Tree

Myself with Others

The Buried Mirror

A New Time for Mexico

The Years with Laura Díaz

Inez

CARLOS FUENTES

Inez

TRANSLATED FROM THE SPANISH BY

MARGARET SAYERS PEDEN

FARRAR, STRAUS AND GIROUX

New York

Farrar, Straus and Giroux
19 Union Square West, New York 10003

Distributed in Canada by Douglas & McIntyre Ltd.
Printed in the United States of America
Originally published in 2001 by Alfaguara, Mexico, as Instinto de Inez
Published in the United States by Farrar, Straus and Giroux
First American edition, 2002

Library of Congress Cataloging-in-Publication Data

Fuentes, Carlos.
[Instinto de Inez. English]
Inez / Carlos Fuentes ; translated from the Spanish by Margaret Sayers Peden.
p. cm.
ISBN 0-374-17553-5 (hc : alk. paper)
I. Peden, Margaret Sayers. II. Title.

PQ7297.F793 I6713
963'.64—dc21

2002020589

Designed by Abby Kagan

www.fsgbooks.com

1 3 5 7 9 10 8 6 4 2

To the memory of my beloved son

CARLOS FUENTES LEMUS (1973–1999)

I have lost, living among humans,
Too many years.
My successive destinies may be read here.
To whom shall I entrust the telling of wondrous successions?

CAO XUEQUIN
The Dream of the Red Pavilion, *1791*

Inez

We shall have nothing to say in regard to our own death."

For a long time this sentence had been going around and around in the aged maestro's head. He did not dare write it down. He was afraid that consigning it to paper would make it real, with fateful consequences. He would have nothing more to say after that: the dead man does not know what death is, but neither do the living. For that reason the sentence that haunted him like a verbal ghost was both sufficient and insufficient. It said everything, but at the price of never saying anything again. It condemned him to silence. And what could he say about silence? He, who had dedicated his life to music—"the least annoying of noises," in the crude phrase of the crude Corsican soldier Bonaparte.

He spent hours concentrating on one object. He liked to imagine that by touching some *thing* his morbid thoughts would dissipate, would cling to the material and physical. He discovered very soon that the price of such displacement was very high. He believed that if death and music identified him (or themselves) too closely as and with an old man with no resources but those of memory, holding on to an object would give him, at ninety-three, earthly gravity, specific weight. Him and his object. Him and his tactile, precise, visible, physical thing: an object of unalterable form.

It was a seal.

Not the disk of wax or brass or lead you find with coats of arms and insignia, but a seal of crystal. Perfectly circular and perfectly whole. It could not be used to seal a document, a door, or a coffer; its very texture, being crystalline, would prevent it from molding to the object to be sealed. It was crystal, sufficient unto itself, with no utilitarian purpose unless that of imposing an obligation, transcending a dispute with an act of peace, determining a destiny, or perhaps certifying an irrevocable decision.

The crystal seal could *be* all these things, although it was not possible to know of what *use* it could be. At times, contemplating the perfect circular object displayed on its tripod near the window, the aged maestro opted for giving it all the traditional attributes—mark of authority, authenticity, approval—without wedding it to any one of them exclusively. Why?

He couldn't say exactly. The crystal seal was part of his daily life and thus easily forgotten. We are all both victims and executioners of the short-term memory that lasts no more than thirty seconds and that allows us to go on living without becoming prisoner to every event that happens around us. But long-term memory is like a castle built of great blocks of stone. It takes only a symbol—the castle itself—to remind us of all its contents. Could this round seal be the key to his own personal dwelling? Not the physical house where he was living in Salzburg; not the transitory houses he had lived in throughout his itinerant profession; not his childhood house in Marseilles, tenaciously forgotten so that he would not have to recall, ever again, the migrant's poverty and humiliation; not even the cave, our first castle, we can reconstruct in our imagination. Could it be the original space, the intimate, inviolable, irreplaceable circle that contains us all but at the price of exchanging sequential memory for an initial memory that is complete in itself and has no need to consider the future?

Baudelaire evokes a deserted house filled with moments now dead. Is it enough to open a door, uncork a bottle, take down an old suit, for a soul to come back to fill it?

Inez.

He repeated the woman's name.

Inez.

It rhymed with "regress," Ee-ness, and in the crystal seal the maestro hoped to find the impossible reflection of both: Inez and a return to a time before the years prohibiting his love. Inez. Regress.

It was a crystal seal. Opaque but luminous. That was its greatest marvel. In its place on the tripod by the window, light could shine through it, and then the crystal scintillated. It shot delicate sparks, and illegible letters appeared, revealed by the light: letters of a language unknown to the aged orchestra conductor, a score in a mysterious alphabet, perhaps the language of a lost people, maybe a voiceless clamor that came from a long-ago time and in a certain way mocked the professional artist who was so faithful to the composition that even knowing it by memory he had to have it before his eyes as he directed . . .

Light in silence.

Lyrics without voice.

The maestro had to bow down, had to go to the mysterious sphere and ponder that there wasn't going to be enough time to decipher the message of the signs engraved within its circularity.

A seal of crystal that must have been carved, caressed perhaps, to reach this seamless form, as if the object had been created by means of an instantaneous fiat: *Seal, create thyself! And the seal was.* The maestro didn't know what to admire most about the delicate sphere that at this very moment he held in his hands, fearful that his small and eccentric treasure might shatter, but tempted every moment (and yielding to that temptation) to lay it in one hand and stroke it with the other, as if looking for both a nonexistent flaw and an inconceivable smoothness. Danger altered everything. The object might fall, crack, shatter to bits . . .

His senses, nevertheless, predominated, and blotted out the presentiment. To see and to touch the crystal seal also meant to savor it, as if it were, more than vessel, wine from an eternally flowing stream. To see and to touch the crystal seal was also to smell it, as if its substance, free of any secretion, should suddenly begin to sweat, erupt in vitreous pores, as if the crystal might expel its own substance and leave an indecent stain on the hand that caressed it.

What was lacking, then, but the fifth sensation, for him the most important: to hear, to listen to, the music of the seal? That would be to trace the complete circuit—to close the circle, to circulate, to emerge from silence and hear a music that could only be the music of the spheres, expressly, the celestial symphony that regulates the movement of all times and all spaces, neverending, simultaneous . . .

When the crystal seal began, first very low, very distantly, barely in a whisper, to sing, when the center of its circumference vibrated like a magical little bell, invisible, born of the very heart of the crystal—its exaltation and its soul—the old man felt first a shiver of forgotten pleasure run down his spine, then an unwanted rush of saliva, the uncontrollable drool of a mouth fitted with yellowed dentures, and then, as if gaze were allied to taste, he lost command of his tear ducts, and he told himself that old men should disguise their ridiculous tendency to weep at the least excuse, should cover it with the pious veil of a senility—lamentable, but worthy of respect—that tends to dribble like a wineskin run through too often by the swords of time.

He then took the crystal seal in his fist, as if to choke it as he would an annoying little gerbil, extinguishing the voice beginning to issue from its transparency, though he was fearful of snapping the seal's fragility in his grip, for he was still strong—even if stringy and strung out—accustomed to directing, cuing without a baton, with the pure flourish of a long-fingered bare hand, as eloquent for the full orchestra as for a violin or piano or cello solo, and stronger than the fragile *bâton* he had always scorned because, he said, it's nothing but a little stick, a stage prop that hinders rather than favors the flow of nervous energy that streams from my black curling locks, from my clear brow bursting with the light of Mozart, Bach, Berlioz, as if they, Mozart, Bach, Berlioz, they alone, were inscribing the score upon that brow, and from my eyebrows, beetling but separated by the sensitive, anguished space between them that they—the orchestra—perceive as my fragility, my guilt, and my punishment for being not Mozart or Bach or Berlioz but, rather, the simple transmitter, the conduit: the *conductor* so filled with energy, yes, but so fragile, too, so fearful of being the first to fail, to betray the work, he who has no right to err, but he who—despite appearances, despite a hiss from the audience or a silent recrimination from the orchestra or an attack from the press or a temperamental scene with the soprano or a gesture of disdain from the soloist or the scornful vanity of a tenor or the buffoonery of a bass—least deserves a critic harsher on himself than he himself, Gabriel Atlan-Ferrara.

He himself, looking at himself alone before the mirror and saying to himself, I wasn't up to the task, I betrayed my art, I deceived everyone who depends on me, the audience, the orchestra, and most of all, the composer . . .

He studied himself every morning in the mirror as he shaved, but he could find nothing now of the man he once had been.

Even the space between the eyebrows, which becomes more noticeable over the years, had in him become overgrown and obscured by the uncontrollable eyebrows sprouting in every direction like those of a tamed Mephistopheles, a tangle he deemed frivolous to groom beyond an impatient shoo-fly gesture that had no effect on the grizzled anarchy, so white now it would be invisible were it not for its copiousness. Once those eyebrows had inspired terror: they commanded, they said that the splendor of the Jovian brow and the tossed-back ebony curls should not be misconstrued, while the space between the eyebrows promised chastisement and sculpted the severe mask of the conductor, with its indescribably invasive eyes, like a pair of black diamonds flaunting their pride in being blazing jewels and inextinguishable carbon, its nose of a perfect Caesar, sharp but with the flaring nostrils of a predator on the scent, brutal but sensitive to the slightest odor; and only then was the mouth traced, admirable, masculine, but fleshy. The lips of an executioner and of a lover, which promise sensuality, but only in exchange for punishment, and pain only as the price of pleasure.

Was this he? This tissue-paper effigy crinkled from so much smoothing out of wrinkles, from being folded so many times among garments packed for the long travels of a famous orchestra, forced, in every climate and under every circumstance, to don the uncomfortable work uniform of white tie and tails instead of the envied overalls that mechanics wear when they—yes, they too—wield the precision instruments of their labors?

That had been he. Today his mirror denied it. But he had the good fortune to possess a second mirror, not the old, flaking mirror in his bathroom but the crystalline reflection from the seal displayed on a tripod before the window open to the unchanging panorama of Salzburg, the Germanic Rome, happy in its gentle valley among massive mountains and its division by the river flowing like a pilgrim from the Alps, bringing water to a city that once perhaps, in another time, had submitted to the impressive power of its natural setting, but at the turn of the seventeenth and eighteenth centuries had created a design rivaling nature's, reflecting but also challenging the world. The architect of Salzburg, Fischer von Erlach, with his twin towers and concave façades and his adornments like billowing air and his surprising military simplicity, which accommodated delirious baroque and Alpine stateliness, had invented a second physical, tangible nature for a city filled with the intangible sculpture of music.

The old man gazed from his window up toward the mountain forests and monasteries, and down at eye level to console himself, but he could not avoid—it was an effort—the monumental presence of the cliffs and fortresses sculpted like a pleonasm on the face of Mönschsberg. The sky raced by above the panorama, with no thought of competing with either nature or architecture.

He had other frontiers. Between the city and him, between the world and him, existed this object from the past, which did not vacillate before the course of time but resisted and reflected it. Was it dangerous, a crystal seal that perhaps contained all the memories of life yet was as fragile as they? Looking at it there, displayed on its tripod near the window, between the city and him, the old man asked himself whether losing that transparent talisman would also mean losing memory; would memory itself splinter if, through his carelessness or that of the maid who came in twice a week, or because of a fit of pique from the good Ulrike—his ponderous housekeeper, affectionately called Dicke or sometimes Dumpling by the neighbors—the crystal seal disappeared from his life?

"If anything happens to your little piece of glass, maestro, don't blame me. If it's so important, put it in a safe place."

Why did he keep it there, in plain sight—almost, you might say, unprotected?

The old man had several answers for such a logical question. He repeated them—authority, resoluteness, fate, emblem—and in the end was left with only one: memory. Stored away in a cabinet, the seal would have to be remembered, instead of being the visible memory of its owner. Exposed, it convoked the memories the maestro needed to go on living. He had decided, seated idly at the piano and slowly picking out, almost like a beginner, a Bach partita, that the crystal seal would be his living past, the receptacle of all he had been and done. It would survive him. The mere fact that it was such a fragile object had led him to impose on it the sign of his own life, almost hoping to transform life into an inanimate object: a *thing*. The truth was that in the impossible transparency of the object all the past of this man who was, had been, and, briefly, would continue to be him, would persist beyond death . . . Beyond death. How long was that? That, he didn't know. It wouldn't be important. The dead man does not know he is dead. The living do not know what death is.

"We shall having nothing to say in regard to our own death."

It was a wager, and he had always been a betting man. Once he had left the poverty of Marseilles behind, and once he had decided to reject wealth without glory, and power without greatness, so as to devote himself to a vocation with true power, music, his life had provided him with the solid pedestal of self-confidence. But all these things that made him *him* depended on something that did *not* depend on him: life and death. The wager was that this object, so bound up with his life, would resist death, and that in some mysterious, perhaps supernatural way the seal would maintain the tactile warmth, the sharp sense of smell, the sweet savor, the fantastic sound, and the inflamed vision of its owner's life.

Wager: the crystal seal would break before he did. Certainty—oh yes!—dream, prediction, nightmare, diverted desire, unutterable love: they would die together, the talisman and its owner . . .

The old man smiled. No. This was no scrap of the skin of a wild ass that shrank with each wish granted for and because of its owner. The crystal seal neither grew nor diminished. It was always the same, but its possessor knew that without its changing shape or dimensions all of a lifetime's memories fit miraculously within it, perhaps revealing a mystery. Memory was not an accumulation of matter that eventually, because of sheer quantity, would burst the seal's fragile confines. Memory fit within the object because its dimensions were identical. Memory was not something that overflowed or was shoehorned into the shape of the object; it was something that was distilled, *transformed*, with each new experience. The original memory recognized each new-come memory, offering it a welcome to the place whence, unknowingly, the new memory had originated, believing itself in the future only to discover that it would always be in the past. What was yet to come would also be a memory.

An image—equally obvious—was different. An image has to be exhibited. Only the most wretched miser hides away a Goya, because he fears not robbers but Goya. Because he fears that the painting, displayed—not even on the wall of a museum, but on a wall in the hoarder's own home—might be seen by others and, worse, might see them. To cut off that communication, to steal from the artist all possibility of seeing and being seen, to interrupt forever his vital outpouring: ah, nothing could be more satisfying to the consummate miser, nothing so near the pleasure of a dry fuck. With every viewing, something of the painting is stolen.

The old man had never, not even when young, wanted to withhold. His arrogance, his isolation, his cruelty, his conceit, his sadistic pleasure—all the defects attributed to him throughout his career—did not include spiritual constipation or a refusal to share his creation with a live audience. It was legend that he refused to give his art to an audience that wasn't present. That decision was definitive. Zero records. Zero films. Zero radio or, horror of horrors, television broadcasts. He was, also legendarily, anti-Karajan, a man he considered a clown to whom the gods' only gift had been the fascination of vanity.

Gabriel Atlan-Ferrara? No, he never wanted that . . . His "art object"—which was how the crystalline seal was presented to society—was in full view. It had become the property of the maestro only recently, having before that passed through other hands; its opacity had been converted into a transparency penetrated by many old, old gazes, which perhaps survived only within the crystal, paradoxically alive because they were captive.

Was it an act of generosity to exhibit the *objet d'art*, as some said? Was it a seigneurial emblem, a seal for a coat of arms, a simple but mysterious cipher engraved on crystal? Was it a heraldic charge? Had it closed a wound? Or was it nothing more or less than the seal of Solomon, imaginable as the matrix of the great Hebrew monarch's royal authority but also identifiable, more modestly, as a rhizomatous plant with pedunculate, drooping greenish-and-white flowers and clusters of red berries: Solomon's seal?

It was none of these. He knew that, but he had no way to confirm its provenance. He was convinced, from what he did know, that this object had been not crafted but *found.* That it had not *been* conceived, but had *itself conceived.* That it had no price because it had absolutely no value.

That it was something transmitted. Yes, transmitted. His experience confirmed that. It came from the past. It had come to him.

But finally, the reason why the crystal seal was exhibited there, near the window looking out over the beautiful Austrian city, had little to do with either memory or image.

It had everything to do—the old man approached the object—with sensuality.

There it was, near at hand, precisely so the hand could touch it, caress it, feeling with every nerve ending the perfect and exciting smoothness of that incorruptible skin, as if it were a woman's shoulder, the beloved's cheek, a lithe waist, or an immortal fruit.

More than sumptuous cloth, more that a perishable flower, more than a hard jewel, the crystal seal was not affected by wear or tear or time. It was something integral, beautiful, forever pleasing to the eye and to the touch when fingers tried to be as delicate as their object.

The old man was a paper ghost, yet his grasp was as strong as forceps. He closed his eyes and picked up the seal in one hand.

This was his greatest temptation. The temptation to love the crystal seal so much that he would destroy it forever with the power of his fist.

This magnetic and virile fist, which conducted Mozart, Bach, Berlioz like no other—what did it leave but a memory, fragile as a crystal seal, of an interpretation, judged in the moment to be genius and unrepeatable. For the maestro never allowed any of his performances to be recorded. He refused, he said, to be "canned like a sardine." His musical ceremonies would be live, only live, and would be unique, unrepeatable, as profound as the experience of those who heard them, as volatile as the memory those same audiences kept of them. In that way, he *demanded* that if they wanted it they would *remember* it.

The crystal seal was like that, like the great orchestral ritual presided over by the high priest that gave and took away with an incandescent mixture of will, imagination, and caprice. The interpretation of the work is, at the moment of its execution, the work itself. Berlioz's *The Damnation of Faust*, interpreted, *is* the Berlioz work. Similarly, the image is the same as the thing. The crystal seal was thing and it was image and both were identical.

He looked at himself in the mirror and searched in vain for some trace of the young French orchestra conductor renowned throughout Europe, who when the war began broke with the fascist seductions of his occupied country and left to conduct in London, risking the Luftwaffe bombs, a kind of challenge from the ancestral culture of Europe to the beast of the Apocalypse, the lurking and sordid barbaric creature that could fly but not walk, except crawling with its belly flat to the ground and its tits slathered with blood and shit.

Then came the main reason to keep the object in an old man's retreat in the city of Salzburg. He admitted it with an excited and shameful trembling. He wanted to have the crystal seal in his hand so that he could hold it and squeeze it until he destroyed it; hold it the way he wanted to hold her, tighter, tighter, until she choked, communicating a fiery urgency, making her feel that in love—his for her, hers for him, theirs for each other—there was a latent violence, a destructive danger, that was the final homage of passion to beauty. To love Inez, to love her to death.

He dropped the seal, heedless yet fearful. For an instant it rolled across the table. The old man picked it up again, feeling a blend of fear and fondness as vivid as that aroused by the adrenaline rush of watching people jump without a parachute in the Arizona desert, a circus he had sometimes watched with fascination on the television he detested, the passive shame of his aging years. He set the seal back on the little tripod. This was not Columbus's egg, which, like the world itself, could sit on a slightly flattened base. Without support, the crystal seal would roll, fall, shatter . . .

He stared at it until Frau Ulrike—Dicke—appeared, holding his overcoat.

She wasn't really fat, merely clumsy in walking, as if she was dragging, more than wearing, her ample traditional clothing (skirts layered over skirts, apron, thick wool stockings, shawl upon shawl, as if she was never warm). Her hair was white, and it was impossible to guess what color it had been when she was a girl. Everything about her—her bearing, her halting walk, her bowed head—made one forget that Ulrike had once been young.

"Professor, you are going to be late for the performance. Remember, it is in your honor."

"I don't need an overcoat. It's summer."

"Herr Professor, from now on you will *always* need an overcoat."

"You're a tyrant, Ulrike."

"Don't stand on ceremony. Call me Dicke, like everyone else."

"You know, Dicke? Growing old is a crime. You can end up with no identity and no dignity, sitting around in a nursing home with other old people as stupid and disinherited as you." He looked at her affectionately. "Thank you for taking care of me, my dear Dumpling."

"Haven't I said it many times? You are a sentimental and ridiculous old man." The housekeeper feigned a little hop, making sure the coat fell correctly over the shoulders of her eminent professor.

"Bah, what does it matter how I dress to go to a theater that was once the court stables?"

"It is in your honor."

"What am I going to hear?"

"What do you mean, maestro?"

"What are they playing in my honor, devil take it!"

"*The Damnation of Faust.* That's what it says in the program."

"You see how forgetful I've become."

"No, no. We all get distracted, especially all you geniuses." She laughed.

The old man took one last look at the crystal sphere before going out into the dusk along the Salzach River. He was going to walk, his step still steady, needing no cane, to the concert hall, the Festspielhaus, and in his head buzzed a self-willed memory: status is measured by the number of Indians under the chief's command. And he was a chief, he should not forget that, not for a single instant, a proud and solitary chief who was dependent on no one—which was why he had refused, ninety-three years and all, to have someone come pick him up at his home. He would walk, alone and without a cane, thanks but no thanks; he was the chief, not "director," not "conductor," but *chef d'orchestre*, the French expression was the one he really liked—*chef.* He hoped Dicke wouldn't hear; she'd think he was crazy if in his old age he devoted himself to the kitchen. And he? How could he explain to his own housekeeper that directing an orchestra was walking on a knife blade—exploiting the need that some men have to belong to a group, to be members of an ensemble, feeling free because they follow orders and don't have to give them, to others or to themselves? How many do you command? Is status measured by the number of people we command?

Still, he thought as he set out for the Festspielhaus, Montaigne was right: no matter how high you may be seated, you are never higher than your own ass. There were forces that no one, at least no one human, could dominate. He was headed for a performance of Berlioz's *Faust*, and he had always known that the work had escaped both its composer, Hector Berlioz, and its *chef d'orchestre*, Gabriel Atlan-Ferrara, and had installed itself in a territory where it defined itself as the "beautiful, strange, savage, convulsive, and harrowing" master of its own universe and its own meaning, victorious over the composer and the interpreter.

Did the seal, which was his alone, take the place of the fascinating and disturbing independence of the choral symphony?

Maestro Atlan-Ferrara looked at it before leaving for the homage being paid him at the Salzburg Festival.

The seal, so crystalline until now, was suddenly fouled with some excrescence.

An opaque form, dirty, pyramidal, similar to a brown obelisk, began to spread from its center, which only moments before had been perfectly transparent.

That was the last thing he noticed before leaving for the performance, in his honor, of *The Damnation of Faust* by Hector Berlioz.

It was, perhaps, an error of perception, a perverse mirage in the desert of his old age.

When he came home that darkness had disappeared.

Like a cloud.

Like a bad dream.

As if divining her master's thoughts, Ulrike watched him walk down the street along the riverbank and did not move from her post at the window until she saw the figure of the professor, still noble and upright though cloaked in a heavy overcoat in midsummer, reach what she calculated to be the point where he would not turn back and interrupt the secret plan of his faithful servant.

Ulrike picked up the crystal seal and placed it in the center of her held-out apron. She made sure, forming a fist around it, that the object was carefully wrapped in the cloth, and then she whipped off the apron with a couple of efficient, professional tugs.

She walked to the kitchen, where without a second's hesitation she laid the apron with the seal wrapped in it on the rough table stained with the blood of edible beasts and, picking up a rolling pin, began to pound it with fury.

The servant's face grew agitated and inflamed; her bulging eyes were fixed on the object of her rage as if she wanted to be sure that the seal was crushed to bits beneath the savage strength of the strong right arm of Frau Dicke, with her braids threatening to fall loose in a cascade of white hair.

"Swine, swine, swine!" she grunted in a diapason that swelled until it exploded in a harsh, strange, savage, convulsive, harrowing scream . . .

Cry out, cry out with terror, howl like a hurricane, moan like the deepest forest, let rocks crash down and torrents roar, cry out with fear because in this instant you see black horses racing through the skies, bells fall silent, the sun is obscured, dogs are baying, the devil has taken over the world, skeletons have come out of their tombs to hail the passing of the inky steeds of damnation. It's raining blood from the heavens! The horses are as swift as thought, as unexpected as death, they are the beast that has pursued us forever, since the cradle, the ghost that knocks at our door at night, the invisible creature that scratches at our windowpane; cry out, all of you—as if your life depended on those cries!—HELP; pray to the Virgin Mary for mercy, you know in your hearts that she can't save you, that no one can save you, you are damned, the beast is pursuing us, it's raining blood, the wings of nocturnal birds are beating in our faces, Mephistopheles has poisoned the world, and you're singing as if you were in the chorus of a Gilbert and Sullivan operetta!

Think what you're doing! You are singing Berlioz's *Faust*, not to please, not to impress, not even to stir emotions; you're singing to spread fear, you are a chorus of birds of bad omen, you bring a warning, you come to take our nests from us, you come to peck out our eyes and eat our tongues, then you answer, with the last hope of fear, you cry, *Sancta Maria, ora pro nobis*, this nest is ours, and if anyone comes near we will peck out his eyes and we will eat his tongue and we will cut off his balls and we will suck the gray matter from his skull and we will draw and quarter him and feed his guts to the hyenas and his heart to the lions and his lungs to the crows and his kidneys to the boar and his anus to the rats—cry out!—cry out your terror, but stand your ground, defend yourselves, there is more than one devil, that's his deception, he poses as Mephisto but the devil is multiple, the devil is a merciless *we*, a hydra that knows no pity and no limit, the devil is like the universe, Lucifer has no beginning and no end, learn this, comprehend the incomprehensible, Lucifer is the infinite fallen to earth, he is heaven's exile rockbound in the immensity of space, that was his divine punishment, *You shall be infinite and immortal on this mortal and finite earth*, but you, this night, here on this stage in Covent Garden, sing as if you were the allies of God abandoned by God, cry out as if you wished to hear God cry out because his favorite ephebe, his angel of light, betrayed him, and God, caught between laughter and tears—the Bible! what melodrama!—gave the world to the devil so that on this finite rock he could play out the tragedy of exiled infinitude: sing as God's and the devil's witnesses, *Sancta Maria, ora pro nobis, ora pro nobis*, cry *has, has, Mephisto*, drive out the devil, *Sancta Maria, ora pro nobis*, horn, sing out . . . bells, peal . . . assert yourselves, brass, the mortal multitude is approaching, you, chorus, you too are a multitude, a legion to drown out the clamor of the bombs with your voices, tonight in London we are rehearsing during a blackout, and the Luftwaffe bombing is relentless, wave after wave of black birds sweep by streaming blood, endless troops of the devil's steeds are racing through the black skies, the wings of the evil one are beating in our faces, *feel* him, that's what I want to hear, a chorus of voices that will silence the bombs, no more, no less, Berlioz deserves that, don't forget that I am French—*allez vous faire niquer!*—sing until the bombs of Satan are silenced, I will not rest until I hear that—do you understand?—as long as the bombs outside drown out the voices inside, we will stay here, *allez vous faire foutre, mesdames et messieurs*, until we drop with exhaustion, until the fatal bomb falls on our concert hall and, worse than fucked, we are ground into the ground, until you and I together rout the cacophony of the war with the dissonant harmony of Berlioz, the artist who doesn't want to win a war, only drag us down to hell with Faust, because we, you and you and you and I as well, have sold our collective soul to the devil; sing like wild animals seeing yourselves for the first time in a mirror and not knowing you are you, howl like the specter that doesn't recognize itself, like the hostile reflection, wail as if you discovered that your image in the mirror of my music is that of the most ferocious enemy, not the Antichrist, but the anti-you, the anti-father and anti-mother, the anti-child and the anti-lover, the creature with shit and pus under its fingernails that wants to stick its fingers up our assholes and in our mouths and in our ears and eyes, that wants to split open our spinal cords and infect our brains and devour our dreams: cry out like animals lost in the forest, beasts that must howl so that other beasts can recognize them from a distance, shriek like the birds to terrorize the aggressor that wants to take our nest from us . . . !

"Regard the monster you had never imagined, not a monster but a brother, a member of your family, who one night opens the door, rapes us, murders us, and burns down the house we all share . . ."

Gabriel Atlan-Ferrara wanted, at that point in the night rehearsal of *The Damnation of Faust* by Hector Berlioz, that December 28, 1940, in London, to close his eyes and know again the overwhelming yet serene sensation of work that is exhausting but finally accomplished; he wanted the music to flow independently to the ears of the public, even though everything in this ensemble depends on the authoritarian power of the conductor: the power of obedience. One gesture to impose authority. One hand, readying the percussion to announce the arrival at hell, the cello to lower its tone to the murmur of love, the violin to signal a tremolo of coming terror and the horn a dissonant caesura . . .

He wanted to close his eyes and feel the music flowing like a great river carrying him far away, away from the specific circumstance of this concert hall on a night during the London blitz, with German bombs raining down all around, and the orchestra and chorus of Monsieur Berlioz conquering Field Marshal Göring and assaulting the Führer himself with the terrible beauty of horror, saying to him, Your horror is true horror, it lacks grandeur, it's niggardly horror, because you don't understand, you will never be capable of understanding, that immortality, life, death, and sin are mirrors of our universal, internal soul, not your transitory and cruel external power . . . Faust places an unfamiliar mask on the man who doesn't recognize it but ends up adopting it. That is his triumph. Faust enters the devil's territory as if returning to the past, to lost myth, to the land of original terror—man's work, not God's or the devil's, Faust conquers Mephisto because Faust is exiled, expelled, expulsed, master of terrestrial terror, terrorized, interred, and disinterred: the human terrain on which Faust, despite his vicious defeat, forever reads himself . . .

The maestro wanted to close his eyes and think what he was thinking, wanted to say all these things to himself in order to be one with Berlioz, with the orchestra, with the chorus, with the collective music of this great and incomparable hymn to the demonic power of the human being when that human discovers that the devil is not a unique incarnation—*has, has, Mephisto*—but a collective hydra—*hup, hup, hup.* Atlan-Ferrara wanted, moreover, to renounce, or at least believe he was renouncing, the authoritarian power that inevitably made him, the young and already eminent European conductor "Gabriel Atlan-Ferrara," the dictator of a collective ensemble untouched by the vanity or pride that could stigmatize the director, free of Lucifer's sin. Inside the theater, Atlan-Ferrara was a minor god who renounced his powers on the altar of an art that was not his, not his alone but first of all the work of a creator named Hector Berlioz—though only he could conduct, he, Atlan-Ferrara, conduit, conductor, interpreter of Berlioz, and in any case authority over the interpreters subject to his power. Chorus, soloists, orchestra.

His limit was the public. The artist was at the mercy of the audience. Ignorant, vulgar, distracted or perceptive, intransigent connoisseur or simple traditionalist, intelligent but closed to the new, like the public that wouldn't accept Beethoven's Second Symphony, damned by a renowned Viennese critic of the time as "a vulgar monster that furiously slashes its uplifted tail until the desperately awaited finale is reached . . ." And hadn't another celebrated critic, this one French, written in *La Revue des deux mondes* that Berlioz's *Faust* was a work of "disfigurement, vulgarity, and bizarre sounds emitted by a composer incapable of writing for the human voice"? With good reason, sighed Atlan-Ferrara, there were no monuments anywhere in the world to the memory of a literary or music critic.

Situated in the precarious equilibrium between two creations—the composer's and the conductor's—Gabriel Atlan-Ferrara wanted to be borne away by the dissonant beauty of the seductive and yet frightening hell of Hector Berlioz's oratorio. The secret to preserving that equilibrium—and consequently the spiritual peace of the *chef d'orchestre*—is that no one person should stand out. Especially in *The Damnation of Faust*, the voice must be collective in order to inspire the unavoidable fall and damnation of the hero.

But this night during the London blitz, what was it that prevented Atlan-Ferrara from closing his eyes and lifting his arms to direct Berlioz's at once classic and romantic, cultivated and savage cadences?

It was that woman.

That singer who rose above the chorus kneeling before a cross—*Sancta Maria, ora pro nobis; Sancta Magdalena, ora pro nobis*—yes, kneeling like all the other women and yet imperious, majestic, distinct, separated from the chorus by a voice as black as her lidless eyes and as electric as the flaming hair curling like an ocean surf of enervating, magnetic distraction, bursting the unity of the ensemble, as above the sun-orange aureole of her hair and below the nocturnal velvet of her voice she was heard as something apart, something singular, something disturbing that endangered the equilibrium-from-chaos so carefully fashioned by Atlan-Ferrara this night when the bombs of the Luftwaffe were reducing central London to ashes.

He interrupted the rehearsal with a furious, unaccustomed gesture, pounding his right fist into his left hand. A blow so loud that it silenced everything except a passionate voice, not insolent yet insistent, a singer at center stage, standing out yet kneeling before the altar of the Sancta Maria.

Ora pro nobis, the woman's high, crystalline voice filling the space of the stage, the singer possessed or empowered by the very gesture attempting to silence her, the conductor's pounded fist. Tall, vibrant, mother-of-pearl skin, red hair, and dark gaze, the singer disobeyed—disobeyed him and disobeyed the composer, for Berlioz himself would not have tolerated a solitary, narcissistic voice rising above the chorus.

The furious bombardment outside imposed silence—the firebombing that since summer had kept the city in flames, a phoenix reborn again and again from its ashes—although this was neither an accident nor an act of local terrorism but aggression from without, a rain of fire that thundered hell for leather through the skies, recalling the final part of *Faust*; everything gave the impression that the hurricane of the skies was erupting like a rumbling earthquake, up from the entrails of the city, that the thunder was the fault of the earth not the sky . . .

It was the silence broken by the rain of bombs that inflamed Atlan-Ferrara, who unconsciously attributed his rage not to what was happening outside, or to its relation to what was happening inside, but to the rupture of his exquisite musical equilibrium—imposing balance on chaos—by that high and profound, isolated and proud voice "black" as velvet and "red" as fire affirming itself by rising above the women's chorus, solitary as the presumed protagonist of a work that wasn't hers, not because it belonged solely to Berlioz or to the director, the orchestra, the soloists, or the chorus, but because it belonged to everyone, and yet the woman's voice, sweetly obstructive, proclaimed, "This music is mine."

"This isn't Puccini, and you're not Tosca, Mam'selle Whatever-Your-Name-Is!" the maestro shouted. "Who do you think you are? Am I some cretin who can't express himself clearly? Or are you some mental case who can't understand me? *Tonnerre de Dieu!*"

The concert hall was his territory, he knew, and the success of the performance depended on the tension between the director's energy and will and the obedience and discipline of the ensemble under his command. The woman with the electric hair and velvet voice was challenging his authority. The woman was enamored of her own voice, she caressed it, took pleasure in it, and she was conducting it herself: the woman was doing with her voice what the conductor did with the ensemble—dominating it. She defied the conductor. She was saying to him, with her insufferable arrogance, Once you're out of this building, who are you? Who are you when you step down from the podium? And deep inside he was silently asking her, How dare you, from your place in the chorus, display your solitary voice and your beautiful face like that? Why do you show such lack of respect? Who are you?

Maestro Atlan-Ferrara closed his eyes. He was overcome by an uncontrollable desire, a natural, even savage impulse to rebuff and scorn this woman who was interrupting the perfect fusion of music and ritual so essential to Berlioz's dramatic legend. But at the same time he was fascinated by the voice he heard. He closed his eyes, believing that he was being seduced to enter the marvelous trance spun by the music, while in truth he wanted to isolate the voice of this rebellious, unthinking woman—though he didn't know that yet. Nor did he know if, feeling these things, what he wanted was to make the woman's voice his, to appropriate it.

"It is forbidden to interrupt, mademoiselle!" he shouted, because he had the right to shout whenever he wanted, and to see if his thunderous voice, his voice alone, would drown out the sound of the bombing outside. "You are whistling in a church at the moment of the sacrament!"

"I thought I was contributing to the work," she said in her ordinary voice, and he thought the way she spoke was even more beautiful than the way she sang. "As they say, variety never stands in the way of unity."

"In your case, it does," the maestro stormed.

"That's your problem," she replied.

Atlan-Ferrara checked his impulse to ask her to leave. That would be a sign of weakness, not authority. It would look like vulgar revenge, a childish tantrum, or something worse . . .

"Ah, love scorned . . ." Gabriel Atlan-Ferrara smiled and shrugged his shoulders, dropping his arms, resigned, in the midst of the laughter and applause of the orchestra, soloists, and chorus. "Can't be helped," he sighed.

In his dressing room, naked to the waist, toweling sweat from his neck, face, chest, and underarms, Gabriel looked at himself in the mirror and succumbed to the vanity of knowing he was young, thirty-three, one of the youngest *chefs d'orchestre* in the world. Briefly, he admired his aquiline profile, his black, curling mane, the infinitely sensual lips. The dark, gypsy-olive skin worthy of his Mediterranean and Central European hyphenated names. Now he will dress in a black turtleneck sweater and dark wool trousers and will throw on the Spanish cape that gives him the soignée air of a kob, a splendid antelope in prehistoric meadows that would swagger into the street wearing a silver collar like the ruff of a Spanish hidalgo . . .

Nevertheless, as he regarded himself with deep regard (and

liking his likeness), he no longer saw his own vain image; it was being obliterated by that of the woman, a very special woman who dared plant her person in the center of the musical universe of Hector Berlioz and Gabriel Atlan-Ferrara.

It was an impossible image. Or maybe merely difficult. He admitted that. He wanted to see her again. The idea distressed him and pursued him as he strode arrogantly into the night of the German blitzkrieg over London; it wasn't the first war, it wasn't the first terror of the eternal combat of man-is-the-wolf-of-man, but, making his way, as sirens wailed, among the people forming a queue to go down to the underground, he told himself that these bureaucrats with headcolds, bone-tired waitresses, mothers with babies, old men clutching thermoses, children dragging blankets, these Londoners with their weariness and bleary eyes and insomniac skin were unique, they belonged not to "the history of war" but to the specific actuality of *this* war. What was he in a city where more than fifteen hundred people could die in a single night? What was he in a London where bombed-out shops displayed signs proclaiming BUSINESS AS USUAL? What was he, leaving the sandbagged theater in Bow Street, but a pathetic figure captured amid the terror of a rain of ice from a shattered shop window, the whinnying of a horse frightened by the flames, and the red aureole that lit up the crouching city?

He walked toward his hotel on Piccadilly, the Regent's Palace, where a soft bed was waiting, a place to forget the voices he overheard as he cut through the lines for the underground.

"Don't waste any shillings in the gas meter."

"Chinese all look alike, how do you tell them apart?"

"We'll all sleep together, it's not too bad."

"Yes, but next to whom? Yesterday my butcher *touched* me."

"Well, we English know about perversion from elementary school on."

"Thank God the children are in the country."

"Don't be too complacent. Southampton, Bristol, and Liverpool have all been bombed."

"And in Liverpool there wasn't any anti-aircraft defense; why, that's dereliction of duty!"

"It's the Jews who're to blame for this war, as usual."

"They've bombed the House of Commons, the Abbey, the Tower of London. Aren't you surprised when you find you still have a house?"

"*We* know 'ow to take it, mate, *we* know 'ow to take it."

"And we know 'ow to help a buddy, more nor ever, mate."

"More nor ever."

"Good evening, Mr. Atlan," said the first violin, wrapped in a sheet that had little effect against the night cold. He looked like a ghost that had escaped from the *Faust* oratorio.

Gabriel nodded with dignity, but at just that moment he was seized by the most *un*-dignified of urgencies. He needed desperately to urinate. He hailed a taxi to speed his return to the hotel. The taxi driver smiled at him amiably.

"First, gov'ner, I don't know me way around the city anymore. Second, the streets are bang-up with broken glass, and tires don't grow on trees. Sorry, gov'ner. It's too risky where you want to go."

He looked for the first alleyway among the many that weave together Brewer's Yard and St. Martin's Lane, trapping the odor of chips, lamb cooked in lard, and rancid eggs. The city's breath was sour and melancholy.

He unbuttoned his fly, took out his cock, and urinated with a sigh of pleasure.

A musical laugh made him turn and stop in midstream.

She was looking at him with affection, with amusement, with attention. She was standing at the entry to the alleyway, laughing.

Then she cried, *"Sancta Maria, ora pro nobis!"* with the terror of someone pursued by a beast, her face beaten by the wings of nocturnal birds, her eardrums pierced by the sound of hooves racing through skies raining down blood . . .

She was afraid. London, with its underground stations, was undoubtedly safer than this open country.

"Then why do they send children to the country?" Gabriel asked as they careened down the road in his yellow sports car, top down despite the cold and wind.

She wasn't complaining. She tied a silk kerchief around her head to keep her red hair from beating her face like the ominous birds in Berlioz's opera. The maestro could say what he wanted, but, driving away from the capital and toward the sea, weren't they inevitably getting closer to France, to the Europe occupied by Hitler?

"Remember Poe's 'The Purloined Letter'? The best way to hide something is to leave it out in the open. If they come after us, thinking we've disappeared, they would never look for us in the most obvious place."

She didn't have much faith in the *chef d'orchestre*, who was driving the little open car with the same vigor and unbridled concentration he devoted to conducting an orchestra, as if he wanted to proclaim to the four winds that he was also a practical man and not just a long-haired musician, as men like him were called in Anglo-American circles, a synonym for an almost idiotically impractical person.

She turned her attention from the speed, the roadway, her fear, to an appreciation of where she was, allowing herself to feel a plenitude that granted this round to Gabriel Atlan-Ferrara—nature endures as the city dies—and made herself focus on the gardens along the road, the woods and the smell of dead leaves, the fog dripping from the hedgerows. She was assaulted by the sensation that sap, an invincible and nurturing energy boundless as a great river with no beginning or end, was flowing without regard for the criminal madness only human beings introduce into nature.

"Do you hear the owls?"

"No, the car's making too much noise."

Gabriel laughed. "The sign of a good musician is to know how to listen to many things at the same time, and to *pay attention* to them all."

She should listen to the owls. They were not only the night watchmen of the countryside but its scullery maids as well.

"Did you know that owls catch more mice than a good mouser?" Gabriel made this more a pronouncement than a question.

"Then why did Cleopatra bring her cats to Rome?" she asked, but not argumentatively.

She thought that it might be nice to have owls around as zealous housekeepers. But who could sleep with that constant screeching?

During the drive from London to the sea, she gave herself to the vision of a full moon so bright in the night sky that it seemed it was there to aid the German planes in their raid. The moon was no longer an excuse for romance. It was the beacon for the Luftwaffe. The war changed the times of everything, but the moon insisted on counting the passing of the hours, and they, despite everything, continued to act like time, and perhaps even the time of time, mother of hours . . . Without the moon, the night would have been a void. Thanks to the moon, the night was defining its monumentality.

A silver fox ran across the road, swifter than the automobile. Gabriel braked and was grateful for the darting fox and for the moonlight. A faint, whispering breeze floated across the heath of ancient Durnovaria and lightly stirred the straight, slender larches whose soft needles of brilliant green seemed to point toward the splendid moon-flooded amphitheater of Casterbridge.

He told her that the moon and the fox had conspired to halt the blind speed of the automobile and invite them—he got out, he opened the door, he offered his hand to her—to join them at the ruin in the middle of this British grassland, abandoned by Rome, abandoned by the legions of Hadrian, as were the beasts and gladiators who died forgotten in the underground cells of the Casterbridge coliseum.

"Do you hear the wind?" asked the maestro.

"Barely," she said.

"Do you like this place?"

"It surprises me. I never imagined anything like this in England."

"We could drive a little farther, north of Casterbridge, to Stonehenge, where there's a big prehistoric circle more than five thousand years old, and in its center alternating pillars and obelisks of sandstone and ancient blue stones. It's like a fortress of the beginning. Do you hear it?"

"Sorry?

"Do you hear the place?"

"No. Tell me how."

"Do you want to be a singer, a great singer?"

She didn't answer.

"Music is the image of the incorporeal world. Look at this Roman amphitheater. Imagine the millenary circles of Stonehenge. Music can't reproduce them because music doesn't copy the world. You're hearing the perfect silence of the heath, and if you listen sharply the coliseum will act as the sound box of a place without time. Believe me, when I conduct a work like Berlioz's *Faust*, I give up measuring time. The music gives me all the time I need. Calendars are superfluous."

He looked at her with his dark eyes, savage at that hour, and was surprised that in the moonlight the eyelids of this woman listening to him became transparent.

He placed his lips on hers, and she didn't protest, but neither did she respond.

He had rented the house—well, the cottage—before the war, when he was beginning to be asked to conduct in England. It was an opportune decision—the conductor smiled ironically—although I, well, no one could have foreseen how fast France would fall to the invaders.

It was an ordinary little house on the coast. Narrow, two stories, pitched roof, living room, dining room, kitchen downstairs, and two bedrooms and a bath upstairs. And the attic?

"I use one of the bedrooms for storage." Gabriel smiled. "A musician collects too many things. I'm not an old man, but I have a century's worth of stuff, piles of scores, notes, sketches, costume drawings, set maquettes, reference books, whatever . . ."

He looked at her, unblinking.

"You can sleep in the living room."

She was about to shrug her shoulders. He had been blocking her view of the stairway. It was so steep that it looked more like a ladder than a stairway, requiring you to use hands as well as feet to climb, rung after rung—like ivy, like an animal, like a monkey.

She looked away.

"Yes, whatever you like."

He fell silent, then said it was late, there were eggs, sausage, a coffeepot in the kitchen, maybe some stale bread and an even harder chunk of Cheddar.

"No." She shook her head. First she wanted to see the ocean.

"It isn't much." The last thing in the world he would do would be to lose his pleasant smile, but it always held a hint of irony. "The coast here is flat and undramatic. The beauty of the region is inland, the part we drove through tonight. Casterbridge. The Roman amphitheater. The gentle, whispering wind. I like even the most arid parts. It pleases me to know that behind me is a whole backbone of quarries, chalk hills, and centuries of clay. All of it pushes you toward the sea, as if the force and beauty of the English landscape were sweeping you seaward, driving you from a land jealous of its somber, rainswept solitude. Look, there, across from where we're standing. See that treeless little islet, that barren rock? Imagine when it emerged from the sea, or was separated from the land; calculate that not in thousands of years, but millions." He pointed, his arm fully extended. "Now, because of the war, the lighthouse there is blacked out. *To the Lighthouse*!" Gabriel laughed. "No more Virginia Woolf."

But she had a different impression of the winter night and of the blazing beauty of the cold but intensely green forested landscape; she was grateful for the tree-covered lanes, because they protected her from the flaming air, from death from the skies . . .

"The really beautiful coast is in the west," Gabriel continued. "Cornwall, too, is land edged toward the Atlantic Ocean by fields of heather. What happens on that coast is a battle. Rock pushes against ocean, and ocean against rock. As you might suppose, the ocean ends up winning. The water is fluid, and generous in that it's always offering form; the land is hard, and scarred, but the encounter is magnificent. Granite cliffs rise almost three hundred feet above the sea; they resist the Atlantic battering them mercilessly, but in their whole formation is the work of that incessant attack of pounding surf. There are advantages."

Gabriel put his arm across the singer's shoulders. This cold early morning facing the sea. She did not reject it.

"The land defends itself against the sea with its ancient stone. There are caves everywhere. The sand is silvery. They say that the caves were smugglers' dens. But footprints in the sand betray. Best of all, the weather is very mild and the vegetation abundant, thanks to the Gulf Stream, the heating system for Europe."

She looked at him, moving a little away from the embrace.

"I'm Mexican. My name is Inés. Inés Rosenzweig. Why haven't you asked me?"

Gabriel's smile broadened, but it was joined by a frown. "For me you have no name or nationality."

"Please, don't make me laugh."

"Forgive me. You're the singer who rose above the chorus to give me her beautiful voice: singular, yes, but still a little savage, needing to be cultivated . . ."

"Thank you for that. I didn't want sentiment . . ."

"No. Simply a voice that needs to be cultivated, like the English heaths."

"You should see where the mesquite grows in Mexico." Nonchalantly, Inés moved away.

"In any case," Gabriel continued, "a woman without a name, an anonymous creature who crossed my path one night. A woman without age."

"Romantic!"

"And who saw me urinate in an alley."

They both laughed, he longer than she.

"A woman you bring for the weekend and forget on Monday," Inés suggested, untying her kerchief and letting the wind whip her red hair.

"No." Gabriel put his arms around her. "A woman who enters my life identical *to* my life, the equivalent of the conditions of my life . . ."

What did he mean? The words intrigued her, and for that reason Inés said nothing.

They drank coffee in the kitchen. The dawn was slow to come, this December day would be short. Inés began to notice what was around her, the simplicity of the house, the rough whitewashed brick. The few books in the living room—most of them French classics, some Italian literature, several editions of Leopardi, of Central European poets. A broken-down sofa. A rocking chair. A fireplace, and on the mantel the photograph of a very young Gabriel, a late-teenager, maybe twenty, with his arm around a boy who was his exact opposite: quintessentially blond, wide smile, without mystery. The two youths weren't wearing shirts, and the photo stopped at their waists. It was a photograph of a swaggering camaraderie, solemn but proud, with the pride of two people meeting and recognizing one another in their youth, appreciating the unique opportunity to face life head-on together. Never to be separated. Not ever.

In the living room two wooden stools were set apart at the distance—Inés calculated instinctively—of a body lying full-length. Gabriel explained that in rural houses like this in England twin stools were placed where the coffin of the deceased would be set during a wake. He had found the two stools like that when he took the house, and he hadn't moved them, well, out of superstition—he smiled—or maybe not to disturb the ghosts.

"Who is he?" she asked, putting the steaming cup of coffee to her lips without taking her eyes from the photograph, indifferent to the maestro's asides on folklore.

"My brother," Gabriel answered simply, looking away from the funerary stools.

"You don't look at all alike."

"Well, I say 'brother' the way you might say 'comrade.' "

"We women never call each other 'sister' or 'comrade' or things like that."

" 'Love,' 'friend' . . ."

"Yes. I guess I shouldn't press you. Sorry. I don't mean to pry."

"No, no. It's just that my words have a price, Inés. If you want me to talk about myself—want, not press—you'll have to tell me about you."

"All right." She laughed, amused by the way Gabriel had turned things around.

The young maestro glanced around his no-frills cottage and said that if it were up to him there wouldn't be a stick of furniture in it, nothing. In empty houses, echoes are the only things that flourish: voices flourish, if we know how to listen. He came here—he stared deep into Inés's eyes—to hear the voice of his brother . . .

"Your brother?"

"Yes, because most of all he was my companion. Companion, brother, *ceci*, *cela*, whatever . . ."

"Where is he?"

Gabriel didn't just look down. He looked . . . down.

"I don't know. He always liked long, mysterious disappearances."

"Doesn't he keep in touch with you?"

"Yes."

"Then you do know where he is."

"His letters have no date or return address."

"Where are they mailed from?"

"I left him in France. That's why I chose this place."

"Who brings them to you?"

"Here I'm closer to France. I can see the coast of Normandy."

"What does he say in the letters? Oh, I apologize . . . I know you haven't given me permission—"

"Yes, yes, don't worry. Look, he likes to reminisce about our life as teenagers. Mmh, he remembers, I don't know, how he envied me when I asked the prettiest girl to dance and showed her off on the dance floor. He confesses he was jealous of me, but being jealous just means making the person we'd like to have all to ourselves more important. Jealousy, Inés, not envy. Envy is poisonous, pointless, because we want to be a different person. Jealousy is generous—we want the other person to be ours."

"What was he like? He didn't dance?"

"No. He preferred to watch me dance and then tell me he was jealous. He was like that. He lived through me and I through him. We were comrades, can you understand? We had this deep tie that the world rarely understands and always tries to destroy: isolating us in jobs, ambition, women, habits we acquire on our own . . . history."

"Maybe it's best that way, maestro."

"Gabriel."

"Gabriel. Maybe if that wonderful youthful friendship had been prolonged, it would have lost its luster."

"Nostalgia preserves it, you mean?"

"Something like that, maestro . . . Gabriel."

"And you, Inés?" Atlan-Ferrara brusquely changed the subject.

"Nothing special. My name is Inés Rosenzweig. My uncle is a Mexican diplomat in London. Ever since I was little, people have said I have a good voice. I went to the Conservatorio de México, and now I'm in London"—she laughed—"sowing confusion among the chorus of *The Damnation of Faust* and giving the celebrated young maestro Gabriel Atlan-Ferrara fits."

She lifted her coffee cup as if it were a champagne flute. She burned her fingers. She was just going to ask the maestro again, "Who brings the letters?" but Gabriel beat her to the punch.

"Don't you have a boyfriend? Didn't you leave someone behind in Mexico?"

Inés shook her head no, and the movement highlighted the cherry tones in her hair. She rubbed her burned fingers discreetly on her skirt. Just at the thigh. The rising sun seemed to pale with envy as it struck the girl's fiery aureole. But her eyes were for the photo of Gabriel and his brother-companion, a beautiful boy, as different from Gabriel as a canary from a crow.

"What was his name?"

"*Is* his name, Inés. He isn't dead. He's just disappeared."

"But you get letters from him. Where do they come from? Europe is cut off—"

"You talk as if you would like to know him."

"Of course. He's interesting. And very beautiful."

A Nordic beauty very different from Gabriel's Latin looks. Was he really handsome or merely *striking*? Brother? Companion? Inés stopped fretting over the question. It was impossible to look at the photograph without feeling something for this boy: love, uneasiness, sexual desire, intimacy maybe, or perhaps a certain icy disdain. Indifference? No. Not permitted by those eyes clear as lakes never furrowed by any craft, straight blond hair like the wing of a splendid heron, slim muscular torso. The torso of the young blond corresponded to features sculpted so finely that one further touch to the nose, thin lips, or smooth cheekbones might have ruined, even erased them.

This nameless youth merited *attention*. That was what Inés told herself that early dawn. The love the brother or comrade demanded was *attentive* love. Don't let an opportunity slip by. Don't lose focus. Be there for him because he was there for you.

"Is that what this photo makes you feel?"

"I'll be frank with you. It isn't the photo, it's him."

"I'm in it too. He isn't alone."

"But you're here beside me. I don't need a photo to see you."

"And him?"

"He is his image. I've never seen such a beautiful man."

"I don't know where he is," Gabriel concluded, and looked at her with irritation and a kind of embarrassed pride. "If you want, you can believe that I write the letters myself. That they don't come from anywhere. But don't be surprised if one day he shows up."

Inés didn't want to back off or show surprise. It was obvious that one rule of getting along with Gabriel Atlan-Ferrara was precisely to affect normality in every situation except moments of great musical creativity. It wouldn't be she who fed the fire of his domineering creativity, it wouldn't be she who laughed at him when she went into the one bathroom without warning—the door was half open, she wasn't violating any taboo—and found him before the mirror preening like a peacock capable of recognizing its own reflection. The laugh came from him, a forced laugh, as he quickly combed his hair, shrugging his shoulders to express disdain, and explaining:

"I'm the son of an Italian mother. I cultivate *la bella figura.* Don't worry. It's to impress other men, not women. That's the secret of Italy."

She was wearing nothing but a cotton robe she had hastily thrown into a weekend case. He was completely naked, and he walked toward her, excited, and embraced her. Inés held him away.

"I'm sorry, maestro. Do you think I came here, docile as a doe, just to answer your sexual summons?"

"You take the bedroom, please."

"No, the sofa in the living room is fine."

Inés dreamed that the house was crawling with spiders and all the doors were closed. She tried to escape from the dream but was stopped by the walls of the house, which were streaming blood. She couldn't find an open door. Invisible hands knocked on the walls, tap-tap-tap, tap-tap-tap . . . She remembered that owls eat mice. She managed to get out of the dream but still could not distinguish reality. She saw herself walking toward a cliff and saw her shadow stretching across silvery sand. Except the shadow was looking at her, forcing her to run back to the house and through a rose garden where a macabre little girl crooning to a dead animal smiled, revealing perfect teeth that were dripping blood, and looked up at her, at Inés. The animal was a silver fox, newly created by the hand of God.

When she woke, Gabriel Atlan-Ferrara was sitting at her side, watching her sleep.

"It's easier to think when it's dark," he said in a normal voice, so normal that it seemed to be rehearsed. "Malebranche could write only when the curtains were closed. Democritus tore out his eyes in order to be a true philosopher. Only when he was blind could Homer see the wine-dark sea. And only when he was blind could Milton recognize the figure of Adam, molded from clay, calling out to God: ". . . it were but right / And equal to reduce me to my dust . . ."

He relaxed his savage black eyebrows. "No one asked to be brought into the world, Inés."

After a frugal breakfast of eggs and sausage, they went out for a walk by the sea. He in his turtleneck pullover and wool trousers, she in a heavy gray wool suit, with the kerchief tied around her head. He told her, jokingly, that this was capital country for hunting. "If you pay attention, you will see flocks of shorebirds with those long beaks for routing out food, and if you look toward land you'll see red woodcocks searching for their breakfast of heather, red-footed partridges, sleek pheasants, mallards and teal . . . Yet all I have to offer you, like Don Quixote's routine Saturday diet, is 'scraps and scrapings.' "

He asked her to forgive him for what had happened the night before. He wanted her to understand. Every artist sometimes has the problem of not distinguishing between what passes for everyday normality and *creativity*—which is also everyday, and not exceptional. It's a well-known fact that the artist who sits around waiting for "inspiration" dies in the waiting, watching the woodcock wing by, and ending up with a fried egg and half a sausage. For him, for Gabriel Atlan-Ferrara, the universe was alive in every moment and in every object. From a stone to a star.

Inés was gazing with hypnotic, instinctive fascination toward the distant island she could see on the ocean horizon. The moon was late going to bed and was precisely above their heads.

"Have you seen the moon during the day before?" he asked.

"Yes," she replied without a smile. "Often."

"Do you know why the tide is so high today?"

She shook her head, and he elaborated: because the moon was exactly overhead and at the moment of its most powerful magnetic attraction. "The moon makes two orbits around the earth every twenty-four hours and fifty minutes. That's why there are two high tides and two low tides every day."

She looked at him, amused, curious, impertinent, asking him silently, And where is all this going?

"To conduct a work like *The Damnation of Faust* requires me to convoke all the powers of nature. You have to keep in mind the nebula of the beginning, you have to imagine a sun, twin to ours, that one day exploded and scattered into planets, you must imagine the entire universe as one enormous tide without beginning or end, in perpetual expansion, you have to feel pain for the sun, which in some five billion years will be an orphan, with no oxygen, shriveled like a child's deflated balloon . . ."

He talked as if he were conducting, convoking acoustic powers with one arm extended and one fist closed.

"You have to imprison the opera inside a nebula that conceals an object invisible from the outside, the music of Berlioz deep in the luminous center of a dark galaxy. It will reveal its light only through the luminosity of the singing, the orchestra, the hand of the conductor . . . revealed thanks to you and me."

He was silent for a brief moment, and then again he smiled at Inés.

"Every time the tide rises at this point where we are standing on the English coast, Inés, it falls at a place in the world exactly opposite from here. I ask myself, and I ask you, does time appear and reappear the way the tide rises and falls so punctually at two opposite points on the earth? Is history replicated and reflected in the opposing mirror of time, only to disappear and reappear by chance?"

He picked up a pebble and skipped it, swift and cutting, arrow and dagger, across the surface of the water.

"And if at times I'm sad, what does it matter that there's no joy in me if there is joy in the universe? Listen to the sea, Inés, listen with the ear of the music I conduct and you sing. Do we hear what the fisherman or the barmaid hears? Maybe not, because the fisherman has to know how to get the jump on the early bird, and the waitress how to cut an abusive client off short. No, because you and I are obliged to recognize the silence in the beauty of nature that becomes noise when you compare it with the silence of God. That is true silence."

He skipped another pebble.

"Music is the midpoint between nature and God. With luck it connects the two. And along with art, we musicians are intermediaries between God and nature. Are you listening? You're a million miles away. What are you thinking about? Look at me. Don't gaze off into the distance like that. There's nothing there."

"There's an island hidden in the fog."

"There's nothing."

"I'm seeing it for the first time. It's as if it had been born during the night."

"Nothing, I say."

"There's France," Inés said finally. "You told me that yourself yesterday. You live here because from here you can see the coast of France. But I don't know what 'France' is. When I came here, France had already surrendered. What is France?"

"It's my country," Gabriel said, with no change in tone. "And one's country is loyalty or the lack of it. Look, I'm conducting Berlioz because his music is a cultural specific of the territorial specific we called France."

"And your brother, or comrade?"

"Has disappeared."

"He isn't in France?"

"Possibly. Do you realize, Inés, that when you don't have any information about someone you love you imagine him in every possible situation?"

"No, I don't believe that. If you know a person, you know what . . . let's say . . . what his repertory of possibilities is. Dog doesn't eat dog, dolphin doesn't kill dolphin."

"He was very calm as a boy. All I have to do is think of that serenity to believe that it's what destroyed him. His bliss. His serenity." He laughed. "Maybe my excesses are an inevitable reaction to the danger posed by angels."

"Aren't you ever going to tell me his name?"

"Let's say his name is Scholom, or Solomon—Hills, or Hearth. Give him whatever name you want. The important thing about him wasn't the name, but his instinct. Do you understand? I have transformed my instinct into art. I want music to speak for me, although I know perfectly well that music speaks only of itself, even when it demands that we enter it and become a part of it. We can't see it if we stay outside, because then we wouldn't exist for the music."

"Him, talk to me about him," Inés urged impatiently.

"Him. Chaim. Any name that suits you." Gabriel smiled

back at the nervous girl. "He was constantly remaining in his instincts. He'd tediously revise everything he'd just done or said. And that's why it's impossible to know his fate. He was uncomfortable in the modern world, which forced him to reflect, stop, exercise the caution of the survivor. I think he longed for a free and natural world that wasn't burdened with oppressive rules. I told him nothing like that had ever existed. The freedom he wanted was the search for freedom, something that we never achieve but that makes us free as we fight for it."

"You're saying there is no destiny without instinct?"

"No. Without instinct you can be beautiful, but you will also be petrified, like a statue."

"The opposite of you."

"I don't know. Where does inspiration come from, energy, the unexpected *vision* you need for singing, composing, conducting? Do you know?"

"No."

Gabriel opened his eyes with mocking amazement. "And I who always believed that every woman is born with more innate experience than a man can acquire in a lifetime."

"That's called instinct?" said Inés, more calmly.

"No!" exclaimed Gabriel. "I assure you that a *chef d'orchestre* needs more than instinct. He needs more personality, more strength, more discipline, precisely because he isn't a creator."

"And your brother?" Inés insisted, with no fear now of a forbidden suspicion.

"Elsewhere," Gabriel answered simply.

This affirmation opened a broad horizon of free associations for Inés. She kept to herself the most secret one, which was about the boy's physical beauty. She gave voice to the most obvious ones: France, the lost war, the German occupation.

"Hero or traitor, Gabriel? If he stayed in France—"

"Oh, a hero, obviously. He was too noble, too committed. He didn't think about himself, he thought about serving . . . even if simply to resist, without acting."

"Then I can imagine him dead."

"No, I imagine him a prisoner. I would rather think he's been captured. Yes. You know, as boys we were fascinated with maps of the world, and globes, and we'd throw dice to see who won Canada or Spain or China. When one of us won some territory or other, we'd yell and shout, you know, Inés, like those terrible cries in *Faust* I was demanding from all of you yesterday, we'd scream like animals, like screeching monkeys marking their territory and communicating its boundaries to the other monkeys in the jungle. Here am I. This is my land. This is my space."

"Then maybe your brother's space is a cell."

"Or a cage. Sometimes I imagine him in a cage. I'll go further. Sometimes I imagine that he chose the cage himself and has confused it with freedom." Gabriel's dark eyes looked toward the other side of the Channel.

The retreating sea was gradually giving up the land it had won. It was a cold, gray afternoon. Inés was cross with herself for not having brought a muffler.

"I hope that like a captive animal my brother defends his space—by that I mean the territory and the culture of France. Against Nazi Germany. An alien and diabolical enemy."

Winter birds flew by. Gabriel looked at them with curiosity. "Who teaches a bird to sing? Its progenitors? Or are its instincts randomly organized? It inherits nothing, and has to learn everything from scratch?"

Again he put his arms around her, this time roughly, a disagreeable roughness she read as fierce machismo, the decision not to take her back alive to the corral . . . The worst of it was that he disguised it, masked his sexual appetite as artistic zeal and fraternal feeling.

"It's possible to imagine anything. Where did he go? What was his fate? He was the brilliant one. Much more so than me. Then why am I the one to triumph and he the one to lose, Inés?" Gabriel was squeezing her harder, pressing his body against hers but avoiding her face, avoiding her lips. Finally he touched his lips to her ear.

"Inés, I'm telling you all this so you will love me. Understand that. He exists. You've seen his photograph. That proves that he exists. I've seen your eyes when you look at the photo. You like that man. You want that man. Except that he isn't here. I'm the one who's here. Inés, I'm telling you all this so—"

Calmly, she moved away from him, hiding her disgust. He did not restrain her.

"If he were here, Inés, would you treat him the way you're treating me? Which of us would you prefer?"

"I don't even know his name."

"Scholom, I told you."

"Stop making things up," she said, now without hiding the bitter taste the situation left in her mouth. "You're exaggerating terribly. Sometimes I wonder whether men really love us; what they want is to compete with other men and best them . . . You still wear your war paint, you men. Scholom, Solomon, Hearth, Chaim . . . You take advantage."

"Imagine, Inés." Gabriel Atlan-Ferrara became decidedly insistent. "Imagine that you threw yourself off a cliff rising four hundred feet above the sea—would you be dead before you hit the waves?"

"Were you what he couldn't be? Or was he everything you couldn't be?" Inés fired back, angry now, her instinct liberated.

Gabriel's fist was clenched from intense emotion and intense anger. Inés pried open his hand and deposited an object on the open palm. It was a crystal seal, with a light of its own and illegible inscriptions.

"I found it in the attic," Inés said. "I had the impression that it wasn't yours. That's how I got the nerve to offer it to you as a gift. A gift from a dishonest guest. I went into your attic. I looked at the photographs."

"Inés, pictures sometimes lie. What happens to a photograph over time? Do you think a photo doesn't live and die?"

"That's what you said before. With time, our portraits lie. They aren't us anymore."

"How do you see yourself?"

"I see myself as a virgin." She laughed uncomfortably. "A good daughter. Mexican. Bourgeois. Immature. Learning. Discovering my voice. That's why I don't understand why memory comes back when I least desire it. It must be that I have a very short memory. My uncle the diplomat always said that our memory of most things lasts no longer than seven seconds or seven words."

"Didn't your parents teach you anything? To put it a better way, what did your parents teach you?"

"They died when I was seven."

"To me the past is the *other* place," said Gabriel, staring toward the far shore of the English Channel.

"I don't have anything to forget." She moved her arms in a way that wasn't hers, that felt strange. "But I feel an urgency to leave the past behind."

"I, on the other hand, sometimes want to leave the future behind."

The sand absorbed their footsteps.

He left abruptly, without saying goodbye, abandoning her, in wartime, on a lonely coast.

Gabriel raced back through Yarbury Forest and the heath of Durnovaria, until he stopped at a high, square, clod-filled field near the river Frome. From there the coast was no longer visible. The land was like a protective frontier, an unfenced boundary, an outdoor sanctuary, a deserted ruin with no obelisks or sandstone columns. The sky of England moves so swiftly that you can stop but still think you are moving as fast as the heavens overhead.

Only there could he tell himself that he had never learned to distinguish the distance between a woman's abject submission and her absolute purity. He wanted her forgiveness. Inés would remember him as misguided, whatever he did . . . He didn't deny that he wanted her or that he had to abandon her. If only she wouldn't remember him as a coward or a traitor. If only she wouldn't give flesh to the other in the person of Atlan-Ferrara, the companion, the brother, the one who was *elsewhere* . . . He prayed that the young Mexican girl's intelligence, so superior to the concept she seemed to have of herself, would always know to distinguish between him and the other—for he was in today's world, forced to fulfill obligations, to travel, to establish order, while the other was free, could make choices, could give all his attention to her. Love her—maybe even that: love her . . . He was elsewhere. Gabriel was here.

But maybe she saw in Gabriel what he saw in her: an avenue

to the unknown. Making a supreme effort to think clearly, Atlan-Ferrara realized why Inés and he should never have sex. She rejected him because she saw another woman in his gaze. But, equally, he knew that when she looked at him she was seeing someone else. And yet couldn't they, servants of time, be him and be her, be themselves and be others in each other's eyes?

I won't usurp my brother's place, he said to himself as he drove off toward the burning city.

His mouth tasted bitter. He murmured: "Everything seems primed for the farewell. Road, sea, memory, wooden death stools, crystal seals."

He laughed. "The stage set for Inés."

Inés made no effort to return to London. And she did not return to rehearsals for *The Damnation of Faust.* Something held her here, as if she were condemned to live in this house facing the sea. She walked along the seashore and was afraid. With ancestral fury, a battle among the winter birds erupted in the sky. The savage birds were fighting over something, something she couldn't see, but something sufficiently prized to justify pecking each other to death.

The spectacle terrified her. The wind scattered her thoughts. Her head felt like a crystal worn smooth.

The ocean terrified her. She remembered, with terror . . .

The little island terrified her, more clearly defined every time she saw it outlined between the coasts of England and France, beneath a flat-ceilinged sky.

It terrified her to think of starting down the deserted road, lonelier than ever—worse, with its murmuring woods, than the silence of the tomb.

What a strange sensation, to walk beside a man along the shore, each attracted to, each frightened of, the other . . . Gabriel had left, but the nostalgia he had sown in her remained. France, the beautiful blond youth, France and the youth united in the nostalgia Gabriel was able to express openly. Not she. She felt bitter toward him. Atlan-Ferrara had left her with the image of something she could never have. A man that from this time forward she would desire but could never know. Atlan-Ferrara did know him. The face of the beautiful blond youth was his heritage. A lost country. A forbidden country.

Her instinct communicated to her an insurmountable separation. A prohibition now stood between her and Atlan-Ferrara. Neither wanted to violate it. But prohibition violated Inés's instinct. Alone, mulling over these things, on the way back to the house, she felt trapped between two temporal boundaries that neither of them wanted to cross.

She went into the house and heard the stairs creaking, as if someone were going up and down, impatiently, uninterruptedly, not daring to show himself.

Then, once back in the house facing the sea, she lay down between the two funerary stools, stiff as a corpse, her head on one support and her feet on the other, and upon her breast the photograph of the two friends, comrades, brothers, signed *To Gabriel, with all my affection.* Except that the beautiful blond youth had disappeared from the photo. He was no longer there. Gabriel, bare-chested, one arm held open, was alone. That arm wasn't embracing anyone. Inés placed two crystal seals on her transparent eyelids.

After all, it wasn't difficult to lie there, stiff as a corpse, between the two funerary stools, buried beneath a mountain of dream.

You will stop and look at the sea. You will not know how you got here. You will not know what you are supposed to do. You will run your hands over your body and it will feel sticky, smeared from head to toes with the same viscous substance that will coat your face. You will not be able to clean yourself with your hands because they too will be covered. Your hair will be a tangled, filthy nest and a thick paste will dribble down into your eyes, blinding you.

When you wake you will be perched among the branches of a tree with your face cradled against your knees and your hands covering your ears to block out the screeches of the capuchin monkey that will club to death the serpent that will never reach the leafy branches where you will be hiding. The capuchin will be doing what you would like to do yourself. Kill the serpent. Now the serpent will not prevent you from climbing down from the tree. But the strength the monkey will reveal as it kills the serpent will frighten you as much as the threat of the snake, or maybe more.

You will not know how long you will have been here, fem, living alone beneath the jungle canopy. There will be moments when you will not be able to think clearly. You will put a hand to your forehead every time you try to weigh the difference between the threat of the serpent and the violence with which the capuchin will kill it but not kill your fear. You will make a great effort to think that first the serpent will threaten you, and that that will happen *before, before,* and the capuchin monkey will club it and kill it, but that will happen *after, after.*

Now the monkey will lope away with an air of indifference, dragging the heavy stick and making noises with its mouth, moving its tongue the color of salmon. The salmon will swim upriver, against the current: that memory will illuminate you, you will feel happy because for a few instants you will have remembered something—although the next instant you will believe that you have only dreamed, imagined, foreseen it. The salmon will swim against the current to give and to win life, to leave their eggs, to await their hatch . . . But the capuchin will kill the serpent, that will be certain, as it will also be certain that the monkey will make noises with its mouth as it completes its work, and the serpent will be able to do no more than hiss something with its forked tongue, and it will also be certain that now the animal with spiky bristles will approach the motionless serpent and begin to strip away its jungle-colored skin and devour its moon-colored flesh. It will be time to climb down from the tree. There will be no danger now. The forest will protect you forever. You will always be able to return here and hide in the thicket where there is no sun . . .

Sun . . .

Moon . . .

You will try to articulate words that serve what you see. The words are like a circle of regular movements that hold no surprise but have no center. One moment when "jungle" will be identical to itself and will be covered with darkness and only the changing sphere the color of the wild boar's back will penetrate some branches. And that other moment when the jungle will fill with rays like the swift wings of birds.

You will close your eyes in order better to hear the one thing that will be with you if you continue to live in the forest, the murmurs of birds and hissing of serpents, the meticulous silence of insects and chattering voices of monkeys. The terrifying incursions of the boars and the porcupines in search of carcasses to strip.

This will be your refuge and you will abandon it reluctantly, crossing the frontier of the river that separates the forest from the flat, unknown world, which you will move toward pushed by something that is not anxiety, lethargy, or remedy, but the impulse to know what is around you while maintaining the absence of *before* and *after*, you who will live *now*, *now*, *now* . . .

You who will swim across the turbulent, muddy river, washing off the second skin of the dead leaves and ravenous fungi that will cover you as long as you live in the branches of the tree. You will come out of the water coated with the dark mud of the riverbank, to which you cling desperately, battling the trembling of the earth and the force of the river in your struggle until you find yourself, on all fours, totally spent, on the opposite shore, where you will fall asleep without ever having stood.

The earth's trembling will wake you.

You will look for a place to hide.

There will be nothing beneath the dingy sky, a sky like a level, opaque ceiling of reverberating stone. There will be nothing but the plain before you and the river behind you and the jungle on the other side of the river and on the plain the herd of gigantic hairy quadrupeds making the earth ring with their hooves and scattering in every direction the troops of panicked reindeer that will abandon the field to the aurochs until the earth grows still and it is dark and the plain sleeps.

This time the incessant scrabbling of the ugly small creature with the pointed nose will wake you as it pokes into the ground rooting out and devouring all the crawling, wiggling little things it can cram into its mouse-spider snout. Its shriek is nearly inaudible, but it is joined by many just like it, until there is a sea of milling, restless, dissatisfied shrews, prophets of a new trembling that will shake the plain.

Perhaps the shrews will hide and the reindeer will return, tranquil now, first displaying themselves, circling on the plain but marking it out into spaces, which other antlered hordes approach only to be aggressively chased off by the lord of that piece of earth. A ferocious battle will take place between the proprietary deer and those disputing its territory. You, hidden, invisible and unimportant to them, will watch that combat of bloodied antlers and penises engorged in the frenzy of combat until one animal establishes itself as master of that space and expels the bleeding vanquished, and in every neighboring space only the beast with the greatest rack and the greatest penis will take possession of the field where now, tame and indifferent, the females of the herd will come to graze and be mounted by the triumphant deer, never lifting their heads or interrupting their grazing, the males puffing and snorting like the accursed heavens that will damn them to eternal combat in order to enjoy this instant, the females silent to the end . . .

And at the end, you alone in the following darkness, crying out alone, as if the antlered herd and their females were still occupying the plain as solitary as you, fem, will be, sensing that you will have to flee from this place, go far away from here, obscurely fearful that an enormous antlered beast will surprise you calmly eating plants by the riverbank and will be confused by your strange scent and your red mane and your four-footed, loping gait . . .

Suns later . . . You will stop and look at the sea. You will not know what to do now. You will feel yourself and find your body sticky, smeared from head to toes with the same viscous substance that will be coated on your face and on hands that will not clean you because they will be coated too and your head will be a tangled, filthy nest, and a thick paste will dribble down into your eyes and blind you. You will wish and not wish to see.

Two sea-dwellers, as long as two *yous* laid end to end, will roil the sea with their battle, at times feinting and at times direct and lethal, now that the two fish use their mouths the way the monkey will use its club, attacking with sharp teeth. This you will see.

You will not understand why they battle in this way. You, hom, will feel abandoned and lonely and sad when you walk along the rocky beach and you find small fish on the rocks identical to the large ones but for their size, their bodies mangled and the mark of the teeth of the large fish imprinted on them like the symbols—and like a light from the sky that memory will return—scratched with stone in the protective hollows in the mountainsides.

You will see the largest fish attack each other in the ocean until one is killed or flees, and you will think you understand that battle but not the death of the fish-babies murdered by their own progenitors—you will see them attack their young again and again—abandoning them, dead, on the beaches . . .

Other times, those same large white lighthearted fish will frolic in the waves, making gigantic leaps and taking the sea as their playground. You will seek a way to have thoughts, feeling that if you think you will have to remember. There will be things you do want to remember and others you would like, or that you will need, to forget.

Forget and remember, facing the sea, there will be two moments in your head difficult to tell apart—instinctively you will put a hand to your forehead every time you think this—because until very recently there will have been no before or after for you, fem, only this, the moment and the place where you will find yourself doing what you will have to do, losing all your memories the more you begin to imagine that one day you will be a different age, you will be small like those dead little fish, you will live close to a protective woman, all that you will forget, fem, at times you will believe that you have done all these things this very minute on this rocky beach, that you will not do anything before or after this moment—it will take a great effort for you to imagine "before" or "after"—but this dark morning with an opaque sun, you will watch the large white fish leap, see them frolic in the sea after killing their offspring and abandoning them on the beach, and for the first time you will tell yourself that this cannot be, this will not be, feeling something flooding inside you like the waves where the lighthearted, murderous fish will be playing.

Then something within you will drive you to move along the beach, twisting and writhing, lifting your arms, clenching your fists, shaking your breasts, parting your legs, squatting as if you were going to give birth, or urinate, or let yourself be loved.

You will cry out.

You will cry out because you will feel that what your body wants to say here by the sea and the game of the white fish and the death of the slaughtered fish will be too violent and impulsive if you do not express it somehow. You will feel this: you will rage explosively while summing up what must happen to you—the monkey will again kill the serpent, the serpent will again be devoured by the porcupine, you will climb down from the tree and you will cross the river; panting, you will fall asleep, and you will wake on the drum of the plain, where the herds of hairy aurochs will scatter and the deer will skirmish to establish their territory and mount their females, and you will wake by the sea watching the fish fight each other and kill their offspring and then happily play—if you do not cry like the bird that you will never be, if you do not give voice to a strange song, throaty and guttural, if you do not cry out to say that you are fem, alone, that the movements of your dance will not be enough, that you will long to go beyond your gestures and say something, shout something beyond your instantaneous gestures by the shore, that you want to shout and sing passionately something that says you will be here, present, available, you . . .

For a long time, alone, you will wander across the solitary land fearing that no one is like you, fem . . .

"Long time" is very difficult to think, but when you say those two words you will always see yourself living beside the immobile woman, in one place and in one moment.

Now, as soon as you begin to walk, you will feel bad that you are not with anyone, and this will fall into your life with the force of brutal abandonment, as if everything you see, feel, or touch is not true.

Now there will be no protective woman. Now there will be no warmth. Now there will be no food.

You will look about you.

There will be only what surrounds you, and that will not be you, because you will be only what you would like to be again.

You will go back toward the trees, because you will be hungry. You will understand that need brought you from the jungle to look for sustenance, and that now the same need will send you back into the thicket with empty hands. You will be thirsty, and you will have learned that the sea where the lighthearted fish will always be playing does not calm you. You will return to the muddy river. On the way you will find blood-colored fruit that you will devour, and then later you will find your hands stained. You will realize that you will walk, eat, stop, and sleep in silence.

You will not understand why you repeat the dance by the sea now, the impetuous movement of body, hips, arms, neck, knees, fingertips . . .

Who will see you? Who will pay attention to you? Who will send the anguished call, the call that will finally be torn from your throat when you run to plunge again among the trees? You are raked by thorns, you are panting as you come out onto a new barren clearing, you run uphill, summoned by the heights of a rock cliff, you close your eyes to relieve the length and the pain of the climb, and then a cry will stop you, you will open your eyes, and what will you see at the edge of the precipice? The cliff sliced away, with emptiness at your feet. A deep ravine, and on the other side, on a high white stony shelf, a figure that will shout to you, that will wave both arms in the air, that will jump up and down to catch your attention, that will say with every movement of his body but especially with the strength of his voice: Stop, don't fall, danger . . .

He will be naked, as naked as you. Something will happen to you for the first time. You will see another moment in which both of you will be covered, but not now, now nakedness will identify you, and he will be the color of sand, all over, skin, body hair, the hair of his head; a pale man will shout to you, Stop, danger, and you will understand the sounds—*eh-dé*, *eh-mé*, *aidez*, *aimez*, help, love—that are rapidly transformed in your look and your gestures and your voice into something that only in this moment, as you call to the man on the other side, you will recognize in yourself: He is looking at me, I am looking at him, I am calling to him, he is calling to me, and if there were no one there where he is standing I would not have cried out, I would have shouted to frighten a flock of black birds or out of fear of a beast lurking in ambush, but now I will call for the first time to ask something of or thank that other being like me but different from me, and now he will not call out of necessity, he will call because he wants to, *eh-dé*, *eh-mé*, help me, love me . . .

You will want to thank him for the cry that kept you from falling into empty space and crashing onto the rock mass at the bottom of the cliff, but since your voice does not carry to him if you do not shout and you do not know how to call the man who will save you, you will have to call more loudly if he is to hear you from the other side of the void, but the sound that will come from your breast, your throat, and your mouth to thank him is a sound you will never have heard during all those moons and suns that spill over you suddenly at the sound of your voice, your solitary wandering finally ended thanks to a cry that you yourself would be slow to call a "cry" if cry were only an immediate reaction to pain, surprise, fear, hunger . . .

Now, when you shout, something unforeseen will happen. Now you will not raise your voice because you need something but because you want something. Your cry will no longer be an imitation of what you will have always heard: reeds rustling in the river, a wave breaking, a monkey announcing its location, a bird preparing to leave the cold far behind, deer bawling as leaves begin to fall, bisons molting when the suns last very long, the rhinoceros easing the folds of its hide into the water, or the boar devouring the remains of carcasses discarded by the lion . . .

Farther and further, you will know that he will answer with very brief sounds, not like the warbling of the birds or the bellowing of the aurochs—*ah aaaaah, o, oooooh, em emmmm, e, eeeeee*—but you will feel a warmth in your breast, you will first call it "feel you are more than him," then "same as what he can come to be," you put together the short sounds *ah-o, ah-em, ah-nel, ah-nel,* that simple cry across the void, above the animal skeletons lying at the bottom of the cliff in the cemetery on the rocks; you will cry out, but now your cry will be something else, it will not be the need of before, there will be something new, *ah-nel,* that simple cry joined to a simple gesture that will consist of opening your arms and then folding them across your breast with your hands open, and then offering those extended hands to the man on the other side, *ah-nel, ah-nel,* and of that voice and that gesture will be born something different, you will know that, but you will not know what to name it, perhaps if he helps you, you will come to give a name to what you are doing . . .

You will feel hunger, and you will pick the small red fruit that will be growing in a nearby forest. But when you return to your place on the edge of the cliff, it will be night, and you will lie down and sleep, as you will have done forever.

Except that, this night, there will be ghosts in your sleep that you will never have dreamed of before. A voice will say to you: You will be again.

When the sun rises, you will get up, agitated because you will fear you have lost him. What you will search for will be the presence of the man separated from you by the abyss.

There he will be, raising his arm, waving.

You will answer in the same way.

But this time he will not shout. He will do the same as you in the afternoon.

He will speak more softly, he will repeat *ah-nel, ah-nel,* pointing to you and then, with his finger pointing to his own chest, he will say with a new, gentle, unfamiliar strength, *neh-el, neh-el . . .*

At first you will not know how to answer, you will feel that your voice will not be enough, you will repeat the moments by the sea, the contortions of your body, and he will only watch you, not imitating you, with a strange gesture of disapproval, distant or distanced; he will cross his arms, he will lift his voice, *ah-nel, ah-nel,* you will understand, you will stop dancing, you will repeat, in your voice, higher but also softer, the song of the birds, the sound of the sea, the swaying trees, the playful monkeys, the battling reindeer, the running river; the sounds will join together, strung together one after another like something that someone will wear around his neck, something, someone, you will be fem protector, fem forgotten, fem that must be found again.

Ah-nel.

That will be you.

You will repeat it, and you will say, I will be me, he will say I am me.

He will point to a path, but his voice will check yours with another voice closer to flesh than to earth, you will hear in the voice of the man—*neh-el?*—a call to the voice of the skin.

A carnal song. A song. How will the word be said that now will not be just a cry?

Song.

Now it will not be just voice.

You will say those words, and the shrieks will be left behind, the screeches, the bawls, the waves, the storms, the grains of sand.

He—*neh-el?*—will climb down the rock, making an inviting gesture that you will imitate, making disconcerting cries that will orient you both, forgetting in your visible urgency to meet the gentle modulations of the names *ah-nel* and *neh-el* and, unable to avoid it, regressing to grunt, howl, and caw, but both feeling in the rapid trembling of your bodies that now, in order to come together more quickly, in order to meet, you both must move from where you are, and in the hurrying toward the encounter so desired now by both, there will be a return to earlier cries and gestures, but it will not matter, and in saying *ah-nel* and *neh-el* you will also have said *eh-dé* and *eh-mé*, and that will be the good part, but you also will have done something terrible, something forbidden: you will have given another moment to the moment you are living and are going to live, you have distorted time, you have opened a forbidden field to *what you already lived before.*

This scene will send you back to the before and after you longed for. There you will re-create how first the reindeer will have paraded themselves, staking out territory beneath the steadily rising sun, prowling about the plain, gathering in large numbers, until combat erupts amid streaming sweat and salt-colored slaver and inflamed eyes and crashing antlers, and you flat on the ground of the plain, longing for the protection of the trees, and the antlered beasts battling all day until there are only as many left as you can count on your hands, each the possessor of a section of the plain.

This sensation will be so vivid that it will dissipate instantly, as if its profound truth will not tolerate lingering reflection. The moment will drive you both to act, to move, to call out.

But both violent action and inarticulate cry will be lost at the moment when, in the dust that will be like the valley floor between the two mountains that will have separated you, you and he will look at one another, will contemplate one another, and then each will shout individually, will move individually, and you will raise your arms and leave your footprints in the dust, then, squatted down, both of you tracing circles with your fingers until physical action is exhausted and you regard one another intently, saying first wordlessly, *eh-dé*, *eh-mé*, we will need each other, we will love each other, and now we will never be what we were before we met.

"Will it . . . be again?" she will venture with words first very low, then lifting her voice, until she is repeating what both one day will call a "song." *Has, has . . .*

Then he will offer you a crystal stone and you will weep and you will press it to your lips and then you will place it between your breasts and that will be your only adornment.

Has, has, merondor dirikolitz, he will say.

Has, has, fory mi dinikolitz, you will reply, singing.

Now, exhausted, you will sleep together at the base of the cliff. But he will stretch out on his back, rigid, and you will go back to your only position for sleeping, curled up on your side, your knees pulled up close to your chin, and neh-el offering his extended arm for you to rest your head on.

Dawn will come, and the two of you will walk together; he will guide you, and now it will not be as it was when you walked alone. Now the way you once walked will seem clumsy and ugly, because by his side your body will move with a different rhythm, which will begin to seem more natural to you. You will return to the seashore, and you will be aware that once again your movements are violent and impetuous, as if something inside you wanted to burst out, but not now, the hand of neh-el will calm you, and the sounds that come from your mouth will resonate with the new emotions you feel thanks to the man's rhythm.

You will walk together and you will look for water and food in silence.

The two of you will move forward haphazardly, not in a straight line but guided by your sense of smell.

At the edge of the plain you will come across the cadaver of a deer at the moment that a lion will be moving away, still devouring the soft viscera of the antlered beast. Neh-el will rush to tear off pieces of what will be left of the gutted body, making signs to you to help take everything the impatient lion forgot, first the remaining fatty parts immediately behind the shoulder bone, a square, dry bone that neh-el will clutch to his chest with one hand, scrambling away from the spoils, and the two of you will hide in the underbrush moments before the boar will appear to devour the discarded remains of the reindeer, russet in time of rut.

Carrying the bone, neh-el will lead you to the cave.

You will go through forests and meadows growing as tall as your line of sight and past swift, roaring rivers before you reach the entrance to a shadowy space.

You will go in the dark through a passage that he will know, you will stop, and neh-el will rub something in the darkness, and then a silver, thorny torch will cast trembling light on the walls, giving life to figures that he will point out to you and that you will stare at with startled eyes, your breast thudding.

They will be the same deer of the plain of combat, two of them, but not as you remember them, the male haughty and proprietary and pugnacious, the female submissive and indifferent.

These two beasts will be facing, mating, he lowering his antlered head toward hers, she lovingly offering him hers, he licking her forehead, the male dropped to his knees, the female lying facing him.

The image in the cave will leave you astounded, ah-nel, and you will weep, seeing this thing that first will cause you amazement but then will force you to think of something you will have lost, forgotten and needed always, and at the same time something you will want to have forever, grateful to neh-el for bringing you here to experience this bewilderment before something that will be so new for you that you will not be able to attribute it to the hands that release yours to take up their task again.

The fat torn from the deer will make the thorny torch flare.

It will burn slowly, trembling, making the amorous figures of the deer seem to move, it will prolong their tenderness, which is identical, ah-nel, to the strange emotion that now will cause you to speak, trying to find the words and the rhythm that celebrate or reproduce or complete the painting—you cannot explain it—which neh-el will continue to sketch and color with fingers smeared with a color like dried blood, like the hide of the deer.

You will feel agitated and happy, allowing something inside you to take form in your voice, things you will never have imagined, a new strength that will begin in your breast and rise to your lips and emerge, resonant, to celebrate everything that pulses within you, things you have never suspected.

What will emerge will be a song, though you have not imagined it. It will be a song filled with all the things you will not know about yourself until this moment: it will be as if all that you will be living—among the trees, near the sea, on the lonely plain—will now come out naturally in tones of strength and tenderness and longing that will have nothing to do with cries for help or hunger or terror; you will know that you have a new voice and that it will be a nonessential voice; something in it, in the voice itself, will lead you to know that these things you will sing as he paints the wall will not be essential, like looking for food or catching birds or protecting yourself from boars or sleeping curled in a ball or climbing trees or tricking monkeys.

What you will sing will no longer be a cry of need.

Farther along you and he will look at one another as you rest, and both of you will know that now you will be together because you will listen to each other and you will feel and see yourselves united forever, you will recognize yourselves as two who will think as one because one will be the image of the other, like those deer that he will paint on the wall while you sing, moving from him to sketch with your hand on the other wall the shadow of the man trying to tell you with the new words of your song that this will be you because this will be me because this we shall be together and because only you and I will be able to do what we are going to do.

You will go out, both of you, every day to look for sharp stones or to find outcroppings where you can break away smaller rocks to carry back to the cave and sharpen there.

You will find remains of animals—the plain will be a gigantic graveyard—and you will harvest what the other animals will always have left: marrow bone that neh-el will heat to extract food that will be yours alone because the other animals will never know about it.

You will also look for the leaves and herbs you will use for food and for curing fevers and aches in your head and body and for cleaning yourself after you defecate or for drying the blood of a wound, things that he will teach you to do, although it will be he who will return naked and wounded from combats that he will never describe to you, who will be leaving the cave less and less frequently.

One day you will not bleed with the waning moon, and neh-el will hold out his hands before you, shaped like a vessel, and say that he will be here to help you. Everything will be fine. It will be easy.

Then will come long, cold nights during which everything that can be accomplished through action will be achieved, now thanks to the rest and silence of the night.

You will learn to be and to rejoice lying side by side, giving voice to the happiness of being together.

"O merikariu! O merikariba!"

Neh-el will rest his head on your swollen belly.

He will say that another voice is coming.

Both of you will be discovering different tones because love will keep changing and sex too will be different and will begin to seek different voices to accompany it.

The songs that will come one after another will be more and more free until your pleasures and desires blend together.

The gestures of need and of song will now be the same.

More and more often neh-el will have to go out alone, and

you will feel his need to look for food as a separation that will make you mute, and this you will tell him, and he will answer that in order to hunt an animal he must be silent. But in his forays he will hear the songs of many birds, and the world will always be filled with tones and cries and also moans.

"But above it all, I will hear your voice, ah-nel."

He will tell you that he will bring fish from the shore but that the water is drawing back and that he will have to go farther and farther to collect clams and oysters. Soon he will be within sight of another land, which will be very foggy and far from the beach of the leaping, murderous fish. But now distant things will seem much nearer.

He will tell you that this will frighten him because without you he will live alone but also with others.

Neh-el will go out to look for food in solitude, and for that he will not need to speak. All that will be needed is to take what is there, he will say. That is why he will return with such haste and alarm to the cave, knowing that there he will see you, he will be with you.

"Merondor dirikolitz."

You will ask him if when he goes out alone he will feel the same as you do, that when alone you need only take what is there, or do what you must do, and thus everything will disappear as soon as it is done or taken.

There will be no sign.

There will be no recollection.

Yes, he will agree, together maybe we will be able to remember again.

You will be surprised to hear that. You will not have realized that little by little you will begin to remember, that in your solitude you will have lost that custom, and that without neh-el your voice will be many things, but especially it will be the voice of suffering and the cry of pain.

Yes, he will agree, I will cry out when an animal attacks but I will be thinking about what I will feel for you until I get back here, and what I will tell you will be the voice of my body hunting and of my body loving.

This I will owe to you, ah-nel. (*Ah-nel, tradioun*)

Neh-el . . . I am going to need you. (*Neh-el . . . trudinxe*)

You will tell me when. (*Merondor aysko*)

Always. (*Merondor*)

That is why the night when her song—your song, ah-nel—will become one prolonged *aaaaaaaaaaaaaaaaaa* and all the pain to come will return to your brain and your body and you will be asking for help as you did at the beginning and he will give it to you, neither of you will say more than what is needed to ask for help, but the looks you will exchange will say that as soon as need is overcome pleasure will return, you found it and you are not inclined to lose it now you have known it, this you will tell the man who prevents you from giving birth to your young as you would wish, you alone, ah-nel, lying back and reaching to receive the child yourself, with the pain that you will expect as natural but with pain added that will not be natural, that will hurt you from the effort you will make to receive your young yourself, with no help from anyone, as you will have done forever and ever. Before.

No—neh-el yells—not that way, ah-nel, not that way . . . (*Caraibo, caraibo*)

And you will feel hatred for the man, he will have brought you this enormous pain and now he wants to take from you your instinct to give birth by yourself, bending down over yourself, you and only you receiving the fruit of your womb, pulling from yourself the tiny bloody body as the females of your tribe will always have done, and he preventing that it be you, preventing your being like all the females of your blood, he forcing you to lie back, to distance yourself from the birthing of your own young, he will slap you in the face, he will insult you, he will ask you if you want to break your back, this is not how man's child is born, you are a woman, not an animal, let me take our child into my own hands . . .

And he will force you to take your anxious hands away from your sex, and it will be he who takes the baby girl into his hands, not you, who are agitated, feverish, upset, eager to take the infant from her father so that it will be you who licks her and cleans away the first skin of mucus and cuts the umbilical cord with your teeth, until neh-el seizes the girl from you to tie the cord and bathe her with clean water brought from the white foaming ravines.

The deer on the walls will forever continue their lovemaking.

The first thing that neh-el will do when he takes the girl from your avid teat will be to carry her to the wall of the cave.

There he will imprint the open hand of a tiny girl on the cool wall.

There the mark will remain forever.

The second thing that neh-el will do is place around the girl's neck the leather thong that holds the crystal seal.

Then neh-el will smile and, laughing, will nip his daughter's buttock.

He had always loved people who were open to surprise. Nothing bored him more than predictable behavior. A dog and its tree. A monkey and its banana. In contrast, a spider and its web: doing the same thing but never repeating . . . It was like a repertoire. A *Bohème* or a *Traviata* produced only because it pleases the public, without considering that it's unique music, irreplaceable . . . and surprising. Cocteau's famous "surprise me" was for him something more than a simple *boutade*. It was an aesthetic. Let the curtain rise over Rodolfo's mansard or Violetta's salon and we see them for the first time.

If that didn't happen, opera didn't interest him and he joined the legion of its detractors: opera is a monstrosity, a false genre that evokes nothing in nature; it is, at best, "a chimerical assemblage" of poetry and music in which both poet and composer mutually torture one another.

With *The Damnation of Faust*, he always had the advantage. However often it was repeated, the work surprised him, his musicians, and the audience. Berlioz possessed a boundless power to astonish. Not because the music was interpreted differently by different ensembles on each occasion—that happened with every piece of music—but because the work itself, Berlioz's choral symphony, was always presented *for the first time.* Previous performances didn't count. More accurately: they were born and they died in the act. The next voice was always the first, and yet the work was laden with its past. Or perhaps on each occasion there was an unacknowledged past?

This was a mystery, and one he didn't want to unveil; then it would cease to be a mystery. The way he interpreted *Faust* was the conductor's secret: he himself didn't know. If *Faust* were a detective novel, at the end no one would know who the murderer was. There was no guilty butler.

Perhaps these were the reasons that led him that morning to Inez's door. He did not arrive in innocence. He knew several things. She had changed her real name for a stage name. She was no longer Inés Rosenzweig, she was Inez Prada, a name with more resonance than consonants; it was more "Latin," and, most of all, it was easier to display and read on a marquee:

INEZ PRADA

In nine years the London member of the chorus had moved up to mastery of *bel canto.* He had listened to her recordings—now the old fragile 78 rpms had been replaced by the novelty of 33⅓ LP (a technical advance that was a matter of indifference to him, because he had vowed that no interpretation of his would ever be "canned")—and he conceded that Inez Prada's reputation was well deserved. Her *Traviata*, for example, was new in two ways, one theatrical, the other musical, but both biographical in the sense of giving Verdi's character a dimension that not only enriched the work but made it unrepeatable . . . for not even Inez Prada could deliver more than once the sublime scene of Violetta Valéry's death.

Instead of using her voice to leave this world with a plausible high C, Inez Prada gradually extinguished it (*E strano / Cessarono / Gli spasmi del dolore*), passing from her arrogant but already ravaged youth of rounds of toasts, to erotic happiness, to the pain of sacrifice, to the nearly religious humbleness of her agony, climaxing, as she gathers all the moments of her life, not in death but in old age. The voice of Inez Prada singing the last scene of *La Traviata* was the voice of a very ill old woman who in the minutes before her death compresses her entire life, summarizes it, and leaps to the years that fate forbade her: old age. A woman of twenty dies as an old woman. She lives what she could not live, given the immediacy of death.

In mi rinasce—m'agita
Isolito vigore
Ah! Ma io ritorno a vivere . . .

It was as if Inez Prada, without betraying Verdi, picked up the macabre beginning of the novel by Dumas *fils*, when Armand Duval returns to Paris, looks for the courtesan Marguerite Gautier in her home, finds her furniture being auctioned, and learns the terrible news: she is dead. Armand goes to Père Lachaise, bribes the guard, locates the tomb of Marguerite, who had died several weeks earlier, bursts the locks, opens the casket, and is confronted with the putrefying corpse of his wondrous young lover: her face green, her open mouth crawling with insects, the sockets of her eyes empty, her greasy black hair plastered to her sunken temples. The living man throws himself upon the dead woman with passion. *Oh, gioia!*

Inez Prada conveyed this beginning of the story while performing its end. It was her genius as an actress and a singer, fully revealed in a Mimi without sentimentalism, inextricably entwined in the life of her lover, preventing Rodolfo from writing, a woman-limpet clamoring for attention, and in a Gilda ashamed of her jester father but shamelessly dedicated to the seduction of the Duke, her father's patron, anticipating with cruel delight the well-deserved pain of the unhappy Rigoletto . . . Heterodox? No doubt, and much criticized because of it. But her heresy, Gabriel Atlan-Ferrara had always thought as he listened to her, restored the Greek root to the word: *haireticus*, he who chooses.

He had admired her in Milan, in Paris, and in Buenos Aires. He had never gone backstage to greet her. She had never known that he was listening and watching from afar. He let her develop her heresy fully. Now both of them knew that they were going to see each other and work together for the first time since the 1940 blitz in London. They were going to meet again because she had requested him. And he knew the professional reason. The Inez of Verdi and Puccini was a lyric soprano, the Marguerite of Berlioz a mezzo-soprano. Normally Inez would not sing that role. But she had insisted. "My vocal register hasn't been fully explored or put to the test. I know I can sing not only Gilda and Mimi and Violetta, but Marguerite as well. But the only man who can develop my voice and conduct me is Maestro Gabriel Atlan-Ferrara."

She did not add, "We met in Covent Garden when I was singing in the chorus of *Faust*."

She had chosen, and he, arriving at the door of the singer's apartment in Mexico City that summer of 1949, was also choosing, heretically. Instead of waiting for the scheduled rehearsal of

The Damnation of Faust in the Palacio de Bellas Artes, he took the liberty—perhaps committed the imprudence—of arriving at Inez's door at noon, knowing absolutely nothing of her situation—would she be sleeping? would she have gone out?—with the idea of seeing her in private before the first rehearsal, planned for that same afternoon.

The apartment was in a labyrinth of multiple stairways with numbered doors on different levels of a building called La Condesa, on Avenida Mazatlán. He had been told it was a favorite place for Mexican painters, writers, and musicians—and also for European artists driven to the New World by the European hecatomb. The Polish Henryk Szeryng, the Viennese Ernst Röhmer, the Spanish Rodolfo Halffter, the Bulgarian Alexis Weissenberg—Mexico had given them refuge. And when Bellas Artes invited the very unsociable and demanding Atlan-Ferrara to direct *The Damnation of Faust*, Gabriel accepted with enthusiasm, as homage to the country that had welcomed so many men and women who could easily have met their death in the ovens of Auschwitz or the typhoid of Bergen-Belsen. By contrast, the Distrito Federal was Mexico's Jerusalem.

For one simple reason, he didn't want his first meeting with the singer to be at a rehearsal. They had a history, a private misunderstanding that could be resolved only in private. It was a matter of Atlan-Ferrara's professional egoism. This way, they would avoid the predictable tension of their first meeting since that predawn morning he had abandoned her on the Dorset coast, from which she had never returned to the rehearsals at Covent Garden. Inez disappeared, only to resurface in 1945 in a famous debut at the Chicago Lyric Opera, giving a different life to Turandot through the trick—Gabriel had to laugh—of binding her feet in order to walk like a true Chinese princess.

Obviously, Inez did not owe her improved voice to this clever device, but North American publicity soared like Chinese fireworks, and once aloft, there it stayed. From that moment, naïve critics happily repeated the popular line: to interpret *La Bohème*, Inez Prada contracted tuberculosis; she holed up for a month in the underground passageways of the Giza pyramid before singing *Aida*; and she turned tricks in order to convey the pathos of *La Traviata*. The Mexican diva neither denied nor confirmed these publicity releases. Everyone knows that in the world of the arts there is no such thing as bad publicity, and Mexico, after all, was the land of mythomaniacs: Diego Rivera, Frida Kahlo, Siqueiros, and maybe Pancho Villa . . . Perhaps a poor and devastated country demanded a full coffer of fascinating personalities. Mexico: hands empty of bread but a head filled with dreams.

Surprise Inez.

It was risky, but if she didn't know how to deal with him, he'd be in command, as he had been in England. Or if she behaved like the *diva divina* she was, the equal of her former maestro, Berlioz's *Faust* would gain in quality, in good, creative, shared tension.

There would be none—the thought surprised him as he stood with knuckles poised to knock—of the conventional language he detested, because it was so inadequate for expressing passion. The voice that represents desire is the stuff of opera—all opera—and he was gambling by knocking at his singer's door.

But he did knock, decisively, and as he did so he told himself he had nothing to fear. Music is the art that transcends the ordinary limits of its own medium: sound. Knocking at the door was itself already a way of going beyond the obvious message (Open up, someone is looking for you, someone is bringing you something) to the unexpected message (Open up, see the face of surprise, let in a turbulent passion, an uncontrollable danger, a harmful love).

She opened the door in a bath towel hastily wrapped around herself.

Behind her was a dark-skinned, completely naked young man with a stupid expression, bleary-eyed, dazed, defiant. He had tousled hair, a scrawny beard, and a thick mustache.

The rehearsal that afternoon was everything he had expected—or more. Inez Prada, as the protagonist Marguerite, was very close to miraculous: she allowed glimpses of a soul lost when the world strips it of passions, passions that Mephistopheles and Faust offer her—and that are as attainable as Tantalus's fruit.

Thanks to this affirmative negation of herself, Inez/Marguerite demonstrated Pascal's truth: uncontrolled passions are like poison. Dormant, they are vices, they feed the soul, and the soul, deceived, or believing it is being nourished, is in fact being poisoned by its own unknown and unruly passion. Is it true, as other heretics, the Cathars, believed, that the best way to rid oneself of passion is to bring it into the open and indulge it, with no restraint of any kind?

Together, Gabriel and Inez succeeded in giving physical visibility to the invisibility of hidden passions. Eyes could see what the music, in order to be art, had to hide. Atlan-Ferrara, rehearsing almost without interruption, felt that had this work been poetry instead of music, it wouldn't have to be exhibited, displayed, presented. But at the same time, Inez's sublime voice made him think that through the chink of possible imperfection in the passage from soprano to mezzo-soprano, the work became more communicable and Marguerite more convincing, transmitting the music through its very imperfection.

A wonderful complicity grew between conductor and singer, a complicity in work that was imperfect in order not to become hermetically sacred. Inez and Gabriel were the true demons, who as they prevented *Faust* from closing in on itself made it communicable, amorous, and even dignified . . . They put Mephistopheles to flight.

Did this result have anything to do with the unexpected meeting that morning?

Inez had a lover; Inez wasn't the virgin of nine years ago, when she'd been twenty and he thirty-three. Who took her virginity? That didn't concern him, nor could he attribute the deed to the poor annoyed, insulting, dazed, vulgar young man who had tried to protest the stranger's intrusion and merely earned Inez's peremptory command: "Put on your clothes and get out."

He had been warned about the punctual caprice of summer rain in Mexico. Mornings would be sunny, but around two in the afternoon the skies grew dark as ink, and around four a torrential rain, an Asian monsoon, would descend upon the once-crystalline valley, settling the dust of the dry lakebed and barren canals.

Lying with his hands clasped behind his neck, Gabriel breathed in the new-green smell of dusk. Drawn by the scent of wet earth, he got up and went to the window. He felt satisfied, and that sensation should have put him on his guard; happiness is a momentary trap that disguises stubborn problems and makes us more vulnerable than ever to the blind legitimacy of bad luck.

Now night was falling over Mexico City, but he didn't let himself be deceived by the serenity of the fresh, green scents of the valley. Odors flushed away by the storm were returning. The moon was coming up, slyly, making one believe in its silvery winks. Full one day, waning the next, a perfect Turkish scimitar this night—although the metaphor itself was another deceit. All the perfume of the rain couldn't hide the sculpture of this land Gabriel Atlan-Ferrara had come to without prejudice but also without forewarning, guided by a single idea: to direct *Faust* and direct it with Inez singing, she too directed by him, guided along the difficult path of changing her vocal range.

Standing there, he watched Inez sleep, naked, on her back, and he asked himself if the world had been created only so those breasts could be known—full like moons but with no danger of waning or eclipse—and the waist that was the gentle and firm coast of the map of pleasure, the mound of shining curls between her legs that was the perfect announcement of persistent loneliness, penetrable only in appearance, defiant as an enemy that dares desert only to deceive and capture us over and over. We never learn. Sex teaches us everything. It's our fault that we never learn, and again and again fall into the same delicious trap.

Maybe he could compare Inez's body to opera itself. Making visible what the absence of the body—body we remember and body we desire—gives us visibly.

He felt tempted to cover Inez's exposed sex with the sheet that had been thrown aside, catching light like that from an Ingres or Vermeer open window. He stopped, because tomorrow at rehearsal the music would act as veil for the woman's nakedness, the music would fulfill its eternal mission of hiding certain objects from view in order to deliver them to the imagination.

Would music steal words as well, not merely vision?

Was music the great mask of paradise, the true fig leaf of our shames, the final sublimation—beyond death—of our mortal visibility: body, words, literature, painting? Was only music abstract, free of visible ties, the purification and illusions of our mortal bodily misery?

He was watching Inez sleep after the lovemaking he had coveted ever since she had sunk into oblivion and hibernated for nine years in his subconscious. Love as passionate as unpredictable. Gabriel didn't want to cover her, because he understood that in this instance modesty would be a betrayal. One day very soon, next week, Marguerite would be the victim of the passion of her body, seduced by Faust through the cunning of the great procurer, Mephistopheles, and when she was snatched from hell by the choir of angels that would carry her to heaven, Atlan-Ferrara, given his wish, would opt for *daring* in his production of Berlioz, he would have the heroine ascend to heaven *naked*, purified by her nakedness, defiant in her beauty. I sinned, I pleasured, I suffered, I was forgiven, but I will not renounce the glory of my pleasure, the integrity of my freedom as a woman to enjoy sex, I have not sinned, you angels know it, you may be carrying me to paradise grudgingly but you have no choice but to accept the sexual joy I found in the arms of my lover; my body and my pleasure have triumphed over the diabolical pacts of Mephisto and the vulgar carnal appetite of Faust; my woman's orgasm has defeated two men, my sexual satisfaction has made two men expendable.

God knows it. The angels know it, and that is why the opera ends with Marguerite's ascension during the invocation to Mary, whose face I, Gabriel Atlan-Ferrara, would cover with the veil of Veronica . . . or maybe the hood of the Magdalene.

An organ-grinder began to play not far from the window where Gabriel was gazing into the Mexican night. Following the sudden rain, the streets gleamed like patent leather, and the perfumes of the cloudburst were disappearing before the onslaught of sputtering grease, the pungent scent of griddle-warmed tortillas, and the rebirth of the maize of the gods of this land.

How different these aromas, sounds, hours, and labors from London's—clouds racing the pale sun, the nearby sea scenting the core of the urban soul, and the cautious but determined step of islanders threatened and protected by their insularity, the blinding green of their parks, the waste of a disdainful river that turns its back to the city . . . and despite everything, the acrid odor of English melancholy, disguised as cold and indifferent courtesy.

As if every city in the world made different pacts with day and night, so that nature, briefly but for as long as necessary, might respect the arbitrary collective ruins we call "city," "the accidental tribe," as Dostoyevsky described another capital, the yellow doors, lights, walls, faces, bridges, and rivers of Petersburg.

Inez interrupted Gabriel's musings, picking up the organ-grinder's song from where she lay in bed: "You, only you, are the cause for all my tears, for my disillusion and despair . . ."

He addressed the chorus with the energizing certainty that at forty-two he was among the conductors most in demand on the new musical planet that had emerged from this most atrocious of wars, a conflict that produced the greatest number of dead in all of history. And because of that he would demand of this Mexican chorus—which should at the least have memories of deaths during their civil war, as well as in daily life—that they sing *Faust* as if they too had witnessed the endless chain of extermination and torture and tears and desolation that were like the signature of the world at mid-century; as if they had seen a naked baby screaming at the top of its lungs amid the ruins of a bombed-out railway station in Chungking; as if they had heard the mute cry of Guernica as Picasso painted it, not a cry of pain but a cry for help, answered only by the whinny of a dead horse, a horse useless in the aerial warfare overhead, the war of Berlioz's black birds beating their wings against the faces of the singers, obliging the horses to moan and tremble, and to take flight, manes flowing, like Pegasuses of death, in order to escape the great cemetery the earth was becoming.

In the Bellas Artes production, during the final ride to the abyss, Gabriel Atlan-Ferrara planned to project the film of the discovery of mass graves in the death camps; the terrible, apocalyptic evocation of Berlioz would become visible, skeletal cadavers stacked up by the hundreds, starved, lewd, skin, bone, indecent baldness, obscene wounds, shameful sexes, embraces of intolerable eroticism, as if even in death desire endured: *I love you, I love you, I love you . . .*

"Cry out as if you were going to die loving the very thing that kills you!"

The authorities forbade running the film of the death camps. "A cultivated and very respectable class of Mexican comes to the Bellas Artes," a stupid official who kept buttoning and unbuttoning his parrot-shit-colored jacket had said. "They don't come here to be offended."

On the other hand, "Berlioz's work is really impressive," was the opinion of a young Mexican musician who attended the rehearsals with the never explicit, though obvious, purpose of checking out this conductor with the reputation for being a rebel, in any case a *foreigner*, and as such *suspicious* in the eyes of Mexican bureaucracy. "Let the composer speak to us of the horror of hell and the end of the world in his own way," said the musician-bureaucrat with the particularly Mexican quiet voice and delicacy of manners that were as distant as insinuating. "Why push so hard, maestro? In short, why would you want to *illustrate*?"

Atlan-Ferrara berated himself and agreed with the affable Mexican. He was putting down his own argument. Hadn't he told Inez just last night that an opera's visibility consists in hiding certain objects from view so the music can evoke them without degenerating into simple thematic painting, or into further, though futile, degradation into a "chimerical ensemble" in which conductor and composer mutually torture one another?

"The opera isn't literature," said the Mexican, sucking his gums and teeth in a genteel effort to extract the remains of some succulent and suicidal meal. "It isn't literature, although its enemies would have it so. Let's not make them think they're right."

Gabriel did tell his cordial bureaucrat that *he* was right. Whatever kind of musician he might be, he was a good politician. What was Atlan-Ferrara thinking? Did he want to teach the Latin Americans who had escaped the European conflict a lesson? Did he want to shame them by comparing historical violences?

The Mexican discreetly swallowed the tiny piece of meat and tortilla that had been lodged between his teeth. "The cruelty of war in Latin America is fiercer, maestro, because it's invisible and has no time frame. Besides, we've learned to hide our victims and bury them at night."

"Are you a Marxist?" Atlan-Ferrara inquired, amused now.

"If you mean that I don't seem to be participating in the current anticommunist phobia, you would be right to a point."

"Then can Berlioz's *Faust* be presented here with no justification beyond being what it is?"

"Yes, it can. Don't divert attention from something we understand very well. The sacred isn't alien to terror. Faith doesn't redeem us from death."

"Then you're also a believer?" The conductor smiled in return.

"In Mexico even we atheists are Catholic, maestro."

Atlan-Ferrara stared at the young musician-bureaucrat offering this counsel. This Mexican wasn't blond, distant, slim: absent. He was dark, and warm; he was eating a tortilla with meat, cheese, mustard, and jalapeño peppers, and his intelligent raccoon eyes darted into every corner. He wanted to get ahead, that you could see. He was going to put on weight very fast.

No, it wasn't him, Atlan-Ferrara thought with a certain leaden nostalgia. He wasn't the long-sought, long-desired friend of the conductor's early youth.

"Why did you leave me behind on the coast?"

"I didn't want to interrupt anything."

"I don't understand you. You interrupted our weekend. We were there together."

"You would never have given yourself to me."

"And so? I thought my company was enough."

"Was mine?"

"Do you think I'm that stupid? Why do you think I accepted your invitation? Because my uterus was in an uproar?"

"But we weren't together."

"No, not like now . . ."

"And we wouldn't have been."

"That's true, too. I told you that."

"You had never been with a man."

"Never. I told you that."

"You didn't want me to be the first."

"Not you, not anyone. I was different then. I was twenty. I lived with my aunt and uncle. I was what the French call *une jeune fille bien rangée.* I was starting out. Maybe I was confused."

"Are you sure?"

"I was a different person, I tell you. How can I be sure about someone I no longer am?"

"I remember how you stared at the photo of my friend."

"Your brother, is what you told me."

"The man closest to me. That's what I meant."

"But he wasn't there."

"Yes, he was."

"Don't tell me he was there."

"Not physically."

"I don't understand you."

"Do you remember the photograph you saw on the mantel?"

"Yes."

"He was there. He was with me. You saw him."

"No, Gabriel. You're mistaken."

"I know that photograph by heart. It's the only one I have of the two of us."

"No. You were alone in the photograph. He had disappeared." She looked at him with curiosity, to keep from showing alarm. "Tell me the truth. Was that boy ever in the photo?"

"Music is an artificial portrait of human passions," the maestro told the group under his direction in Bellas Artes. "Have no illusion that this is a realistic opera. I already know that you Latin Americans cling desperately to logic and reason—concepts totally foreign to you—because you want to escape the supernatural imagination that is your heritage—though not inevitable, and especially to be scorned in the light of a supposed 'progress' that you will never achieve, make no mistake, through embarrassing, slavish imitation. For a European, you see, the word 'progress' always, *s'il vous plaît*, appears in quotation marks."

He smiled at the wall of solemn faces.

"Imagine, if it is helpful, that as you sing you are repeating sounds of nature."

His imperious gaze swept across the stage. How well he played the role of peacock! He laughed at himself.

"An opera like Berlioz's *Faust*, especially, can deceive all of us and make us believe we are listening to the imitation of a nature violently pushed to its limits."

He stared hard at the English horn, until the musician was forced to look down.

"This can be true. But musically it's of no value. Imagine, should you find it helpful, that in this terrible last scene you are repeating the sound of a gently flowing river or of a crashing waterfall."

He opened his arms in a large, generous gesture.

"If you like, imagine that your singing is imitating the sound of the wind in the forest, or the lowing of a cow, or the thump of a stone against a wall, or the shattering of some crystal object; imagine, if you like, that you are singing with the whinnying of a horse and the beating of crows' wings."

Crows began to fly, beating against the orangeish dome of the concert hall; lowing cows crowded down the aisles of the theater; a horse galloped across the stage; a rock exploded against the Tiffany-glass curtain.

"But I tell you that noise never reaches our ears in the form of more noise. Everything in the world that's audible must be converted into song, because it is more than guttural sounds, and if the musician wants the burro to bray, he must make him sing."

And the voices of the chorus, animated, motivated as he wanted by the enormity of an impenetrable, fierce nature, responded: Only you bring a break to my endless boredom, you renew my strength, I am alive again.

"This isn't the first time, you know, that a group of singers has believed that their voices are an extension of, or a response to, the sounds of nature."

He was silencing them, little by little, one by one, banking the choral fire, cruelly extinguishing it.

"One may think she is singing because she hears a bird—"

Marisela Ambriz plummeted wingless to the ground.

"Another because he imitates the tiger—"

Sereno Laviada purred like a house cat.

"Still another because he hears a waterfall inside him—"

The musician-bureaucrat noisily blew his nose from the orchestra pit.

"None of this is true. Music is artificial. Ah, you will say, but human passions aren't. Let's forget the tiger, Señor Laviada, and the bird, Señorita Ambriz, and the thunder, señor-who-eats-sandwiches-and-I-don't-know-your-name," he said, turning toward the pit.

"Cosme Santos, at your service," the accused replied with automatic courtesy. "Licenciado Cosme Santos."

"Ah, very well, friend Cosme, let's talk about the passion awakened by music. We need to remember that the first language of gestures and cries is manifest as soon as a passion appears that takes us back to when we needed that passion." He ran nervous hands through his black, tousled gypsy hair.

"Do you know why I learn the names of each and every one

of the chorus members?" His eyes opened like two eternal scars. "To make you understand that the common, everyday language of men, women, and animals, is *af*fective; it is a language of cries, orgasms, happiness, flight, sighs, and deep laments."

And the open scars were two black lakes.

"Of course"—now he smiled—"as each of you sings—Señor Moreno, Señorita Ambriz, Señora Lazo, Señor Laviada—as each one of you sings, the first thing that occurs to you is that you are giving voice to the natural language of passions."

Dramatic pause by Gabriel Atlan-Ferrara. Inez smiled. Whom was he fooling? Everyone, no less.

"And it's true, it's true. The passions we keep inside can kill us, blow up inside us. Song liberates them, and finds the voice that characterizes them. So, then, music would be a kind of energy uniting the primitive, latent emotions you would never display when you catch a bus, Señor Laviada, or when you're preparing breakfast, Señora Lazo, or taking a shower—forgive me—Señorita Ambriz. The melodic tone of the voice, the movement of the body in dance, liberates us. Pleasure and desire come together. Nature dictates tones and cries: these are our oldest words, and that is why our first language is an impassioned song."

Gabriel turned to look at the musician, bureaucrat, and perhaps censor. "True, Señor Santos?"

"Of course, maestro."

"*A lie.* Music is not a substitute for natural sounds sublimated by artificial sounds." Gabriel Atlan-Ferrara stopped, and, more than glancing around or staring, his eyes penetrated each and every one of his singers.

"Everything in music is artificial. We have lost the original unity between speech and song. Let us mourn that. Sing a requiem for nature. RIP."

His expression became melancholy.

"Yesterday I heard a plaintive song in the street. 'You, only you, are the cause for all my tears, for my disillusion and despair.' "

If an eagle could talk, it would look like Atlan-Ferrara.

"Was that street singer expressing in music the deepest sentiments of his soul? It's possible. But Berlioz's *Faust* is the complete opposite. Señoras and señores," Atlan-Ferrara concluded, "emphasize the distancing of what you sing. Rid your voices of all sentiment and recognizable passion, convert this opera into an oratorio to the unknown, to words and sounds that have no antecedents, no emotion but their own, in this apocalyptic instant that may be the instant of creation: invert time, imagine music as an *inversion* of time, a song of origin, a voice of the dawn, with no antecedent and no consequence."

He lowered his head with feigned humility.

"Let us begin."

Then, nine years ago, she hadn't wanted to yield to him. She had waited for him to come and yield to her. He had wanted to make love to her on the English coast, and had stored forever ridiculous sentences for a moment he imagined or dreamed of or wanted, or all those things at the same time—how would he know?—"We could walk together across the bottom of the sea"—only to find a different woman, one capable of dispatching a casual lover.

"Put on your clothes and get out."

And who was capable of saying that not just to the poor mustached devil, but to him, Maestro Gabriel Atlan-Ferrara. She obeyed him in rehearsals. Even better: they had a perfect understanding. It was as if that arc of Art Nouveau stage lights united the two of them, orchestra pit to stage, in a miraculous meeting between conductor and singer that also energized the tenor, Faust, and the bass, Mephistopheles, drawing them into the magic circle of Inez and Gabriel, as in tune and alike in artistic interpretation as they were at odds and unlike in their carnal relations.

She dominated.

He admitted it.

She had the power.

He wasn't used to that.

He studied himself in the mirror. He had always thought of himself as haughty, vain, swathed in the imaginary cape of a grand gentleman.

She remembered him as emotionally naked. Slave to a memory. The memory of another youth. The boy who didn't grow old because no one ever saw him again. The boy who had disappeared from the photograph.

Through that opening—through that absence—Inez slipped in to dominate Gabriel. He regretted it and he accepted it. She had two whips, one in each hand. With one she said to Gabriel, I have seen you stripped, defenseless before an affection you insist on disguising. With the other she lashed him: You didn't choose me, I chose you. I didn't miss you then and I don't miss you now. We make love to assure the harmony of the work. When the performances are over, you and I will be through, too.

Did Gabriel Atlan-Ferrara know all this? Know it and accept it? In Inez's arms he said yes, he accepted it, in order to have Inez he would accept any arrangement, any humiliation. Why did it always have to be she who mounted him—he on his back and she on top, she directing the sexual game but demanding of him, in his trapped, submissive, prostrate position, all manner of touchings, imperatives, obvious pleasures that he could do nothing but grant her?

He grew used to being the one with his head on the pillow, flat on his back, watching her body rise above him like a monument to the senses, a column of enthralling flesh, a single carnal river from her sex joined to his, to spread thighs, buttocks bucking on his testicles, to hips flowing toward a waist at once noble and amused, like a statue laughing at the world by grace of a similarly amused navel, and finally to the firm but bouncing breasts, flesh merging into a neck of insulting whiteness as the face grew distant, alien, hidden behind the mass of red hair, the mane like a mask of veiled emotion . . .

Inez Prada. ("It looks better than Inés Rosenzweig on the marquees and is easier to pronounce in other languages.")

Inez Revenge. ("I left everything behind me. And you?")

For what? My God, what was she getting even for? ("The prohibition belonged to two different times that neither of us wanted to violate.")

The night of the opening, Maestro Atlan-Ferrara stepped up on the podium amid applause from an expectant public.

This was the young conductor who had drawn such unsuspected sounds—latent? no, lost—from Debussy, Ravel, Mozart, and Bach.

This night he was conducting for the first time in Mexico, and everyone wanted to assess the strength of the personality announced in his photographs: long black curly hair, eyes somewhere between flashing and dreamy, demoniac eyebrows that reduced Mephisto's disguises to comedy, imploring hands that made Faust's gestures of desire seem awkward . . .

They said that he was better than his singers. However, the perfect, evolving, and enviable harmony between Gabriel Atlan-Ferrara and Inez Prada, between lovers with a dual dynamic in bed and onstage, dominated everything. Because, however much she fought for the agreed-on equality, in the theater he imposed his will, he led the game, he mounted her, he subjected her to his male desire, though at the end, at the finale, he placed her in the center of the stage, hand in hand with the child seraphim. Singing beside the celestial spirits, making her aware that, contrary to anything she might suspect, she was always the one who dominated, the center of the relationship that (neither of them could think otherwise) achieved parity only because she was queen of the bed and he master of the theater.

The maestro, conducting the final scenes, quietly spoke the words, *The heavenly virgins will dry the tears, Marguerite, torn from you by earthly sorrows, have hope*, and then Marguerite, who is Inez, holding the hands of the children of the chorus, each holding the hand of another, and the last giving his to a singer in the celestial choir, and this singer to her neighbor, and the next to the next, until all the choir, with Marguerite/Inez in the center, was truly a single choir united by the chain of hands, and then the two angels at either end of the semicircle formed on the stage each held out a hand to the box closest to the proscenium and took the hand of the nearest member of the audience, and this person the one nearest him, and she to the next, until everyone in the Bellas Artes was a choir of hands holding hands, and although the chorus was singing, *Have hope and smile upon your blessings*, the theater was a great lake of flames, and in the depths of every soul a horrifying mystery was taking place: they were all going to hell, they had thought they were climbing to paradise but they were going to the devil; Gabriel Atlan-Ferrara shouted in triumph, *Has! Irimuru kara-brao, has, has, has!*

He was alone in the abandoned hall. As they took their bows, Inez had told him, "I'll see you in an hour. At your hotel."

Gabriel Atlan-Ferrara, sitting in the first row of seats in the empty theater, watched them lower the great glass curtain fabricated over a period of nearly two years by Tiffany craftsmen, a million tiny gleaming pieces fitted together until, like a river of lights emptying into the auditorium, a panorama of the valley of Mexico was formed, with its awesome and loving volcanoes. They faded like the lights of the theater, of the city, of the concluded performance. But, like crystal seals, the lights of the glass curtain continued to glitter.

In his hand Gabriel Atlan-Ferrara held and stroked the smooth shape of the crystal seal Inez Rosenzweig-Prada had put there amid applause from an enthusiastic audience.

He left the auditorium and walked out into the pink marble vestibule, with its strident murals and installations of lustrous copper, all in the Art Nouveau style that in 1934 ended a construction begun with Caesarian ostentation in 1900 and interrupted for a quarter-century by civil war. Outside, the Palacio de Bellas Artes was a great wedding cake conceived by an Italian architect, Adamo Boari, surely with the idea that the Mexican building would be the bride of Rome's monument to King Vittorio Emmanuele: the wedding would have been consummated with marble phalluses and crystal hymens between meringue sheets, except that in 1916 Boari fled from the Revolution, horrified that the lace of his dream was being trampled by the horses of Zapata's and Villa's troops.

It sat there, abandoned, a skeleton of iron, and that was what Gabriel Atlan-Ferrara saw when he left the small plaza in front of the Palacio: naked, stripped, rusting for a quarter-century, a castle of scrap sinking into the rancorous mud of Mexico City.

He crossed the street to Alameda Park, and a black obsidian mask greeted him, making him feel happy. The death mask of Beethoven stared at him with closed eyes, and Gabriel bowed and said good evening.

He walked into the lonely park, accompanied only by words from Ludwig van, talking to him, asking him whether in fact music is the one art that transcends the limits of its own means of expression, which is sound, in order to manifest itself in such sovereign fashion in the silence of a Mexican night. The Aztec city—the Mexican Jerusalem—was kneeling before the mask of a deaf musician capable of imagining the sound of Gothic stone and the Rhine River.

The treetops were swaying softly in the hours after the rain, funneling the docile powers of the heavens from their leaves. Berlioz was behind, still resonating in the marble cavern with his valiant French vowels bursting the prisons of harsh consonants, that "horrid" Germanic articulation structured of verbal armorplate. The flaming sky of the Valkyries was a stage prop. The Faustian hell of black birds and careening horses was flesh and blood. Paganism does not believe in itself, because it never doubts. Christianity believes in itself, because its faith is always being tested. The colonial Inquisition executed its victims in these peaceful gardens of the Alameda, and before that, Indian merchants had bought and sold slaves. Now tall, rhythmic trees covered the nakedness of motionless white statues, erotic and chaste only because they were marble.

The distant organ-grinder broke the silence of the night.

"Only your fatal shadow, the shadow of evil, follows wherever I go."

The first blow landed on his mouth. His arms were pinned to immobilize him. Then the mustached man with the scrawny beard kneed him in the belly and testicles, punched him in the face and chest, as Atlan-Ferrara tried to focus on the statue of the woman kneeling in a posture of anal humiliation, offering herself, *malgré tout,* to the amorous hand of Gabriel Atlan-Ferrara, who was staining her marble buttocks with his blood and trying to understand those foreign words: *cabrón, chinga tu madre,* motherfucker, don't go anywhere near her again, you goddamn ball-less fag, she's my woman . . . *Has, has, Mephisto, hup, hup, hup!*

Was an explanation of his behavior on the English coast required? He could tell her that he always fled from situations in which lovers adopt the habits of an old married couple. The postponement of pleasure is a principle of true eroticism, at once practical and sacred.

"Ah, so you were imagining a bogus honeymoon?" Inez smiled.

"No, I wanted you to have a mysterious and loving memory of me."

"Arrogant and unsatisfied." She stopped smiling.

"Let's just say that I left you behind at the cottage to preserve the curiosity of innocence."

"Do you think you gained something by that, Gabriel?"

"Yes. Sexual union is momentary, and at the same time permanent, however fleeting it may seem. On the other hand, music is permanent, and yet it is short-lived compared with the lasting power of the truly instantaneous. How long does the most prolonged orgasm last? And how long renewed desire?"

"It depends. On whether two are involved . . . or three."

"Were you expecting that at the shore? A *ménage à trois*?"

"You introduced me to a man who wasn't there, remember?"

"I told you, he comes and goes. His absences are never conclusive."

"Tell me the truth. Were you ever that boy in the photo?"

Gabriel didn't answer. He watched the rain washing everything and said he wished it would last forever, take everything.

They spent a blessed night of peace and deep fulfillment.

Only at dawn, Gabriel tenderly stroked Inez's cheeks and felt obliged to tell her that maybe the boy for whom she felt such an attraction would reappear one day.

"Honestly, haven't you ever found out where he went?" she asked, without many illusions.

"I suppose far away. The war, the camps, desertion—there are so many possibilities in an unknown future."

"You say that you used to ask the girls to dance and that he watched and admired you."

"I told you he was jealous of me, not envious. Envy is resentment of the good things that happen to other people. Jealousy increases the importance of the person we wish belonged only to us. Envy, as I told you, is poison, and futile—we want to be the other person. But jealousy is generous—we want the other person to be ours." Gabriel's expression imposed a long pause. Finally he said, "I want to see him to make amends."

"I want to see him so I can go to bed with him," Inez replied without a trace of malice, only icy virginity.

Every time the two of you part, you will cry out: neh-el in the forest growing colder and more deserted, ah-nel in the cave growing less and less warm, to which he will bring skins ripped from the few bisons wandering nearby, animals he will kill not merely to feed you and your daughter but now to robe you against the icy winds filtering through unexpected cracks in the cave like the breath of a white, vengeful ram.

An invisible layer of ice will be forming on the cave walls, as if reproducing there an image of the sickness of the ever more barren and inert earth, as if the blood of animals and the sap of plants were about to shut down forever after spewing a great mouthful of death.

Neh-el will cry out in the winter forest. His voice will have so many echoes that no beast will be able to locate him; his voice will be the disguise of neh-el the hunter. That voice will spread across the blinding white of forests, plains, frozen rivers, and a sea astonished at its own motionless chill . . . It will be a solitary voice that will become multitudinous, because the world will have become one great dome of white echoes.

In the cave, you will not cry out, ah-nel, you will sing, crooning to the girl who soon will have lived three flowering seasons, but in your den of stone your voice will resonate so strongly that the crooning will sound like a cry. You will be afraid. You will know that your voice will always be yours but now will also belong to the world surrounding you with threat. A great downpour of icy rain will resound like a drum in your head. You will look at the paintings on the walls. You will feed the flame of the fire. Sometimes you will venture outside with the hope of finding herbs and berries easy to pick for you and for the girl whom you carry on your back in a pouch of elk hide. You will know that game will always be brought by him, sweating and red-faced from the ever more arduous hunt.

The man will enter the cave, he will look with sadness at the paintings and he will tell you that the time has come to go. The earth will freeze and will give no more fruit or meat.

But, most important, the earth will move. This very morning he will have seen how the mountains of ice are shifting, with a life of their own, slowing as they encounter obstacles, swallowing everything in their path . . .

You will all go out wrapped in the skins that neh-el will wisely have gathered, because it will be he who knows the world outside and who will know this time is coming to an end. But you will pause at the cave entrance and you will run back to the shelter of your life and your love and there you will again sing with the always clearer feeling that it will be your voice that binds you forever to this place, which will always be the hearth of ah-nel and her daughter.

You will sing today as you will sing at the beginning of everything, because in your breast you will feel something taking you back to the stage where you will once again be when you have need of it for the first time . . .

Your feet wrapped in pigskin tied with gut will sink into the deep snow. You will cover the child as if she had not yet been born. You will think that the march is long even though he warns you: We are going back to the sea.

You will expect to find a coast of motionless cliffs and dashing waves, but everything you knew will have disappeared beneath the white robe of the great snow.

You will align your footsteps in the direction of the remembered place of the fish and distressed you will search for the dark line of the horizon, the accustomed limit of your gaze. But now everything will be white, color without color, and everything will be frozen. The sea will not be moving. It will be covered by a great slab of ice, and you will stop, confused, holding your daughter warmly wrapped in skins, watching the group that will be slowly approaching, moving toward you from the invisible limit of the frozen sea as you, you and your daughter, led by neh-el, will go forward to meet the group that will lift their voices with an intent that you will not know how to decipher but that will evoke in the expression of your man an uncertainty about whether to continue forward or to return to the frigid death of the vast shifting ice that is advancing with a life, intelligence, and sinuousness of its own behind you, robbing you of your accustomed hearth, the cave, the cradle, the paintings . . .

The sea of ice will be breaking up like a pile of cold and forgotten bones, but the group of men who will come out to meet you will guide you from block to frozen block until you reach the other shore. Then you will realize that this is the coast or the island that neh-el and you will have seen like a mirage in the old time of the flowers, which will also be the new time awaiting you here, for the men who will lead you will be shedding their heavy mantles of skins cured from the blond deer of the cold to uncover garments of much lighter pigskin. You will have crossed the frontier between ice and green, growing things.

You too will throw aside the heavy pelt you are wearing and you will feel enough warmth return to your breasts to protect your child. You will feel the heat, following the group of men whom now you will begin to tell apart by the way they hold their sharp-pointed lances, together singing a song that will announce triumph, joy, return . . .

You will come to the barrier of a white fence that you will quickly recognize as a wall of the huge bones of vanished animals embedded in the ground to form an impregnable stockade, which, one by one, the men-guides will enter, preceding you, and you will follow through openings in the stockade until you come to a large open area of stamped-down earth amid a cluster of small shelters of baked clay and burning-hot flat roofs.

They will assign you a hut, and they will bring vessels with milk and pieces of raw meat impaled on iron skewers. Neh-el will bow in thanks and will follow the men outside. At the door he will turn and he will tell you with a hand gesture that you must be calm and say nothing. There will be something new in his eyes. He will look at the men of this place the way that before he looked at the beasts he hunted. But now he will also look with suspicion, not caution alone.

You will spend several hours feeding the little girl and crooning songs to her. Then neh-el will return and he will tell you that he will go out every day to hunt with the other men. They are to meet at the edge of a treeless prairie where there will be great herds. They will surprise their kill when the beasts stop to graze. You will go out with the other women to pick herbs and fruit near the huts, without exposing yourself to the beasts that come up almost to the stockade.

You will ask him if here he will paint again. No, he will tell you, here there will be no cave walls. There will be walls of earth and stockades of bone.

Will they be happy to have us?

They will be. They will say that when they see the waters of the sea withdraw and freeze on the other shore, they will feel isolated, and they will wait for us to have proof that the world on the other side still exists.

Will they like our world, neh-el, will they want it?

We shall learn to know them, ah-nel. We shall wait.

But again there will be uneasiness in his eyes, as if something that has not yet happened were about to be revealed.

You will join the other women of the stockade to pick fruit and will bring elk's milk to the little girl in her cradle of skins.

You will not be able to communicate with the other women, because you will not understand their languages; not you theirs or they yours. You will try to communicate by singing and they will answer, but it will not be clear to you what they are saying, because their voices will be unvarying and monotone. You will try to intone voices of happiness, pity, pain, and friendship, but the other women will look at you oddly and they will answer you with the same unvarying tone, which prevents you from divining what they feel . . .

Days and nights will go by in this manner, until one evening, at sunset, you will hear footsteps, so light that they communicate pain, as if the one walking did not want her feet to touch the ground. But the person who will approach your hut will knock with a steady sound that will frighten you because until now the footsteps and noises of this place will have been characterized by a monotonous sadness.

You will not be prepared for the appearance in the frame of your doorway of a woman covered in skins as black as her hair, with deep circles under her eyes and a partly opened mouth: black lips, black tongue, black teeth.

She will clutch the black staff she will use to knock at your door. She will appear at your doorstep, and with one hand she will lift the staff, and you will fear her threat, except that with the other hand she will touch her head with a resignation, a sweetness, and a sorrow that will make your fear vanish. She will touch her head as if she were touching a wall or were announcing herself in a way not to cause fear or because she wanted to greet you, but there is no time, the somber features of the woman, your visitor, will ask something of you, but you will not know how to answer her plea in time, the other women of the community will have reacted, they will come to your door, inflamed, they will yell at the dark woman, they will tear the black staff from her hands, they will throw her to the ground and kick her, and she will get to her feet with darting glances of fear and pride, and, defiant, she will cover her head with her hands and she will leave, dragging her feet, until she is lost in the mist of twilight.

Neh-el will return, and he will tell you that the woman is a widow who has no right to leave her hut.

Everyone will be wondering why, knowing the law, she will have dared go outside and come to you.

They will suspect you.

The law will say that to see a widow is to expose oneself to death, and they will not be able to explain why this widow will have dared come out and go looking for you.

It will be the first time that the other women will lose their calm or their distant indifference, they will change their tone of voice, they will become excited and passionate. The rest of the time, they will be submissive and silent. They will gather the yellow strawberries and the black berries and the white ones, they will pull up edible roots, and they will count with particular care the little green spheres they call *pisa*, opening the green pods and dropping the round fruit into clay vessels.

They will also gather eggs of the birds that flock to feast on grains and the black berries. For their men they will cook the brains, the tripe, and the fat throats of the beasts of the prairie. And as the evening light wanes they will braid rope from the fibers of the fields and make needles of bone and clothing of leather.

You will realize, when you go with the women to distribute food and clothing to the huts of the men and the ill, that, although the scope of this daily, monotonous labor is restricted to the area of the bone stockade, farther away there is a space within a fortress where a building more sumptuous than the others will be built—it, too, of the ivory of death.

One night there will be a great uproar and everyone will run to that space, summoned by the drums that you will have heard before but also by a new music, rapid as the flight of the raptor, only of a sweetness you will never have heard before . . .

The men will have dug a space deeper than wide, and from the large house, yellow as a mouthful of infected teeth, they will carry the body of a naked young man, followed at a slow pace—in its very slowness as much rage as grief—by a man with long white hair and sagging shoulders, his face covered by a mask of stone and his body protected by white hides. He will be preceded by a second young male, as naked as the corpse, carrying a vessel. The men will set the body of the young man on the ground and the old man will go over to look at it, for a moment removing his stone mask in order to take in every detail of the cadaver.

He will have a face that is bitter but lacking the necessary will to contest or to act.

Then the men will lower the body into the hole, and the aged, masked man will slowly empty over it the vessel of ivory pearls the sad adolescent will have in his hands.

Then will rise the song that you will have expected from the beginning, ah-nel, as if everyone were awaiting that one occasion to add to the plaintive chorus the cries, caresses, and sighs that the old man will hear, unmoved, as he sprinkles the pearls over the corpse, and then, exhausted, he will support himself on two men, and all three will return to the house of ivory accompanied by the sound of sad, sweet music issuing from a tube drilled with small holes, while the other men of the stockade will continue to toss objects into the open grave.

That night neh-el will show you something stolen from the tomb. It is the bone tube with many holes. Instinctively neh-el will lift it to his lips, but you, also instinctively, will put your hand over the instrument and over neh-el's mouth. You will be afraid of something, you will suspect even more, you will feel that your days in this place will not be peaceful, ever since the visit from the woman with the staff you will have convinced yourself that this place is not good . . .

There will be a portent in the flight of vultures over the fields where you will be working the morning after the burial of the young man. Neh-el will return with more news. The hunters will have talked, even though the women will have been silent. Neh-el will quickly learn the key words of the language of the island and will tell you, ah-nel, that the boy is the oldest of the old man's sons, that the old man is the one who commands here, that the dead youth was to have been the one to ascend to the ivory throne, the first among all the sons of the *basil,* for that is what the old man is called, *fader basil,* that he has several sons but that they are not equal, that there are a first, a second, and a third, but now the second will be the favorite and the one who will succeed the aged *fader basil.* Terrible things will be said, ah-nel, it will be said that the second son killed the first in order to be first himself, but, then, ah-nel will ask, will not the old man fear that the second will kill *him* in order to be the new *fader basil*?

You must say nothing, ah-nel. I will hear more, and I will tell you.

Will we understand them and they us?

We will. I do not know why, but I think that, yes, we will understand each other.

Neh-el, I am beginning to understand what the women say . . .

Neh-el will stop in the doorway and will turn to look at you with the kind of alarm and amazement that are like the division between inside and outside, yesterday and today.

Standing in the entrance to the hut, with the yellow light at his back, he will say:

Ah-nel, repeat what you just said.

I too understand what the women say.

You understand, or you will understand?

I understand.

You know, or you will know?

I learned. I know.

What do you know?

Neh-el, we have returned. We have been here before. That is what I know.

Now the sky is moving. Swift clouds not only bear wind and noise but are possessed of time; the sky moves time, and time moves the earth. Storm follows storm like lightning, flashing and immediately gone but never preceded by the sound of thunder, the bolts as they fall rip the firmament and rivers run again, forests are inundated with penetrating scents and trees are revived, yellow birds flock, redbreasts, whitetails, blackcrests, blue fantails, plants grow, fruit falls, and later leaves, and again the forests will be denuded, and all this while neh-el and you keep the secret of your resurrected past.

You have been here.

You know the tongue of this place, language returns, but in this moment no one pays attention to you, because the widow of the chieftain's first son has thrown a mantle of black skins over her husband's tomb, hurling curses against the second son, accusing him of killing the firstborn, accusing the aged *fader basil* of blindness and powerlessness, of being unworthy to be *basil*, until the company of men with lances bursts into the open space before the house of bones and a young man with black braided hair, large lips, a darting, furtive gaze, uncompromising gestures, and an attitude of new beginnings, and adorned with large metal bracelets at his wrists and stone necklaces around his neck, gives the order to run the woman through: if she loved her dead husband so much, let her be joined with him forever. He is your brother, the widow manages to shout before she is silenced, bathed in blood.

Blood moistens the earth, and she seems to sink into it and become one with the corpse of her young husband.

I do not want to go out, you say, hugging your daughter. I am afraid.

They will suspect, neh-el answers. Go on working as you have been. As I shall do. Do you remember anything more?

No. Just the language. With the language, the place came too.

I knew, too. I knew that we had been here.

Both of us? Only you?

He was silent for a long while, stroking the little girl's red hair. He stared at the walls of this, his former homeland. For the first time ah-nel saw shame and pain in the eyes of her daughter's father.

I know how to paint only on stone. Not on earth. Or ivory.

Answer me, you say, your voice low and anguished. How do you know that I was here too?

Again he does not speak but goes out as usual to hunt, and returns with a faraway look on his face. Many nights go by like this. You grow more distant, you cling to your daughter as if she were your salvation, you and he do not speak, a silence more confining than any captivity weighs on you both, each of you fears that silence will become hatred, distrust, separation . . .

Finally, one night, neh-el cannot bear it any longer, and he throws himself in your arms weeping, he asks your forgiveness: When memory returns you see that it is not always good, memory can be very bad, I believe we must bless and treasure the not remembering, it was because of forgetting that you and I came together, but also—he tells you—the memories of a man and a woman who meet again are not the same, one remembers some things the other has forgotten, and the other way around, and at times we forget, because the memory is painful, and we must believe that what happened never happened, we forget what is most important because it may be the most painful.

Tell me what I have forgotten, neh-el.

He did not want to go in with you. He led you to the place, but once there he took the girl with the red hair and black eyes from your arms and told you that he would go back to the hut so no one would suspect . . . And to save the girl? you wondered, wanting to ask.

Yes.

You saw a small hillock of baked earth covered by tree branches, hidden by them. This mound had a hole in the top, and many branches overhanging it and thrusting inside. There was another hole at ground level.

That was how you went in, on all fours, taking a while to grow accustomed to the darkness but slowed also by the pungent odors of rotted herbs, discarded pods and husks, old seeds, urine and excrement.

You were led by the rasp of irregular breathing that sounded as if it came from someone caught unawares between wakefulness and sleep, or between dying and death.

When, finally, your eyes adjusted to the shadows, you saw the woman sitting propped against the concave wall, covered with heavy skins and surrounded by ruminants with gray backs and white bellies, companions to the woman, whose smell was strongest of any. You recognized that smell from your life on the other shore, where small herds of musk deer took cover in the caves and filled them with that same secreted scent of nightfall. Fruit peels and gnawed bones were also scattered near the woman.

She was watching you from the moment you entered. Shadow was her light. Motionless, she seemed not to have the strength to move from that hidden place in the forest outside the ivory stockade.

Ah-nel could not see the woman's arms beneath the coverings. The appeal in her eyes was enough to call you to her side. The ceiling was higher in the center than at the sides. You knelt beside her and saw two tears roll down her wrinkled cheeks. She did nothing to brush them away. She kept her arms beneath the skins. You wiped the tears, using the ends of her long wiry white hair to dry the face with gleaming eyes set deep above wide nostrils and a large, half-open, drooling mouth.

You came back, she said to you, her voice trembling.

You nodded yes, but your eyes betrayed your ignorance and confusion.

I knew you would come back. The aged woman smiled.

Was she truly so old? She seemed old because of the wild white hair that hid much of her strange, emotional face. And she seemed old because of her posture, as if her very weariness was proof that she was alive. Beyond the fatigue you had sensed when you saw her, there could only be death.

She told you she could see you clearly because she was used to living in darkness. Her sense of smell was very sharp, her most useful sense. And you would have to speak in a low voice, because living in silence she could hear the most distant murmurs, and loud voices frightened her. She had unusually large ears—she pulled back her hair and showed you a long, hairy ear.

Pity me, the woman said suddenly.

How? you murmured, instinctively obeying.

Remember me. Be kind.

How shall I remember you?

Then the woman pulled a hand from beneath the skins bundled around her.

She extended an arm covered with thick gray hair. She held out a closed fist. She opened it.

In the rose-colored palm lay something ovoid in shape, worn down from constant handling yet still recognizable. You could make out, ah-nel, the shape of a woman with a small, nearly featureless face and an ample body with generous breasts, hips, and buttocks narrowing into legs and tiny feet.

The figure was so old and eroded that it was becoming transparent. The original forms were by now egg-smooth.

She placed the object in your hand without a word.

Then, immediately, she put her arms around you.

You felt her wrinkled, hairy skin against your pulsing cheek. You felt both repulsion and affection. You were blinded by the unexpected and unfamiliar pain from the center of your throbbing head, a pain identical to the effort you were making to recognize this woman.

Then she threw off her covers and softly pushed you until you were lying at her feet, headfirst and on your back, and she opened her short hairy legs and emitted a cry of pain that blended with a cry of joy as you lay on your back, as if you had just been expelled from the woman's womb, and then she smiled and took your arms and drew you to her, and you saw the slash of her sex like a split strawberry, and she pulled you close and kissed you, she licked you, she spit out what she sucked from your nose and your mouth, she guided your mouth to her flaccid, hairy red breasts, then in pantomime she repeated the motion of reaching down to her exposed sex and acted out taking your just-born body in the long arms made for giving birth alone, effortlessly, with help from no one . . .

Satisfied, the woman folded her arms; she looked at you with affection and said to you, Be careful, you are in danger, never say you came here, keep what I gave you, give it to your descendants. Do you have children? Do you have grandchildren? I do not want to know, I accept my fate, I have seen you again, daughter, this is the happiest day of my life.

She got up and moved beside you, on four feet, as you crawled from the dark hovel.

A few steps away, your loving confusion made you turn to look back.

You saw her hanging from a tree branch, waving one long hairy arm, and the last thing you saw was the rosy palm of her hand.

You told neh-el, with tear-filled eyes, that your one labor in this place was to care for your daughter and for the woman in the forest, to serve her, to give life back to her.

Neh-el seized you by the arms and for the first time shook you roughly. You cannot, he told you, for my sake, for yours, for our daughter's, for her own sake, ever say what you have seen, you did not remember her, the fault is mine, I should not have taken you, I let myself be moved by pity, but I remembered, yes, ah-nel, we have different mothers, never forget that, different mothers. Of course, neh-el, I know, I know . . .

Yes, but the same father, the young man with the braided hair, olive skin, and clanking bracelets said that night. Now look at your father. At our father. And tell me if he deserves to be chief, the father, the *fader basil.*

They brought him from the house of ivory, naked except for a loincloth. In the center of the open space was a tree trunk stripped of branches. A greased column, said the man with the braids, to see if our father can climb to the top and demonstrate that he deserves to be chief . . .

The metal rings on his arms clanked, and the old man was freed and led to the column by guards carrying lances.

Sitting on a throne of ivory, the dark young man explained to the young couple from the other shore: The tree is greased with musk, but even without it our lord and father would be unable to put his arms about it and climb. He is no monkey—he laughed—but, more than that, he is weak. It is time to replace him with a new chief. This is the law.

The old man repeatedly put his arms around the greased column. Finally, he capitulated. He dropped to his knees and bowed his head.

The young man on the throne gestured with one hand.

With a single swing of his ax the executioner cut off the old man's head and delivered it to the young one.

He showed the head, holding it aloft by its long white hair, and the community shouted or wept or sang their rehearsed jubilation; you felt the impulse to join in the shouting, to transform it into something more like song. Dimly, you respect those shouts, because you sense that if neh-el recovered his memory because of language, you will recover it only through song, the gestures, the shouts, which inhibit you because you have returned to the state you were in when first you needed them: you fear that you have returned to the conditions of the first time you had to cry out like that . . .

The new chief held the old chief's head by hanks of its hair and showed it to the men and women of the community of the bone stockade. They all sang something and began to disperse, as if they knew the length of the ceremony. But this time the new chief stopped them. He shouted an ugly sound, neither animal nor human, and said that the ceremony did not end there.

He said, The *gods*—everyone exchanged glances, not understanding, and he repeated: the *gods*—have ordered me to carry out their orders this day. This is the law.

He reminded them that the time was approaching for them to send the women away and to deliver them to other villages in order to avoid the horror of having brothers and sisters fornicate and engender beasts that walk on four legs and cannibalize one another. This is the law.

He told them with a dreamlike gaze that some remembered the time when mothers were the chiefs and they were loved because they loved all their children equally, without distinction.

People shouted their agreement, and the young *fader basil* shouted louder than anyone: That was the law.

He warned them they must forget that time and that law—he lowered his voice and opened his eyes very wide—and that whoever said that that time was better and that law better than the law of the new time would have his head cut off, like the useless old father, or run through with a lance, like the weak, moaning widow. This is the law.

He instructed them, showing sharply filed teeth, that this was a new time, in which the father commands and indicates his preference for the eldest son, but if the eldest son prefers pleasure and a woman's love to commanding men, he must die and yield his place to the one who knows how and wishes to command without temptations and on his own. This is now the law. He who commands will live alone, without temptation or counsel.

The young *basil* made a gesture with his arms that brought a great roar from the community.

Then he said, calming the voices, that this was the new order and all must respect it.

When the mother ruled, everyone was equal and no one could stand above another. Individual merit was stifled in the cradle. It was the time of no foresight, of hunger, of a life that blended into everything surrounding it, animal, jungle, mountain stream, sea, rain . . .

That is no longer the law.

Now the time has come for a single chief to organize tasks, rewards, and punishments. This is the law.

Now is the time when the first male son of the chief will in his turn someday be chief. This is the law.

He stopped, and instead of looking at you, as everyone expected, he turned away from you, from your man, and from your daughter.

Brother and sister shall not fornicate together. This has always been the law. The descendants of the guilty brother and sister shall never know carnal pleasure. This is the law. The descendants will pay for the guilt of the parents. This is the law.

Then, in a single unforeseeable instant and with the lethal strike of the lightning bolt, the men in the service of the young chief pinioned neh-el's arms, took the girl from him, jerked her legs apart, and with a stone knife sawed out her clitoris and threw it, ah-nel, in your face.

But you were not there.

You fled from this accursed place, your only possession, clutched in your fist, the small, worn statue of the woman that kept wearing away until it turned into a crystal womb with silhouettes forever etched upon it of the recovered memory of the naked blond man—a memory discovered one ancient night in the dust on the other side of the sea, and of your dark-eyed, red-haired daughter tortured and mutilated by order of a maddened king, a devil posing as a god, and you running far away, shouting and howling with no one pursuing you, they content with your having seen what you saw and you condemned to live forever with that pain, with that rancor, with that curse, with that thirst for vengeance born in you as a song, feeling again the passion that can give birth to a voice, liberating the passion's natural song, allowing the violent external movements of a body on the verge of exploding to be expressed as voice . . .

With your cry you approach the beasts and birds that from now on will be your only companions, again possessed of an impetuous inner tumult to which you give an ululating, jungle, marine, mountain, fluvial, subterranean voice: your song, ah-nel, allows you to flee the brutal turmoil of a life destroyed in one instant for acts that you neither control nor understand but that make you guilty; you add them all up and eliminate the quadruped mother of the forest, the handsome husband who was your brother, the older brother who possessed the power and was dead before dying because of the death he lived in life, the decapitated father stripped of his vigor by life and of his life by the cruel usurping son; you eliminate everyone but yourself, you are the guilty one, ah-nel, you are responsible for the mutilation of your daughter, but you will not go back to ask forgiveness, to get your daughter back, to tell her you are her mother, to keep from passing on to the girl what was passed to you, separated forever from your mother, from your father, from your brothers, from your dead brother, from your abandoned lover . . . So you come back, crossing the frozen sea, to the beach of your meeting, and from there to the frozen valleys, and from there to the cave painted by neh-el, and there, ah-nel, you fall to your knees and press your mother's hand to the mark left one day by the hand of your newborn daughter, and you weep, you swear that you will find her, that she will be yours again, that you will steal her from the world, from power, from deceit, from cruelty, from torture, from men, that you will wreak revenge on all of them in order to fulfill your maternal duty to your daughter and live with her the life you cannot have today but will have one day in the future.

She dreamed that the ice was beginning to recede, uncovering rugged boulders and deposits of clay. New lakes have formed in the mountain sculpted by the snow. There is a new landscape of striated rocks, and flocks of stone. Beneath the ice of the lake an invisible storm is brewing. The dream is forming into a chain. Memory becomes a cataract that threatens to drown her, and Inez Prada wakes with a cry.

She isn't in a cave. She's in a suite at the Savoy in London. She casts a sideways glance at the telephone, the hotel notepad and pencils, to reassure herself. Where am I? An opera singer often doesn't know where she is or where she's just come from. This place, however, resembles a luxurious cavern, everything is chromed and nickeled, the bath, chair backs, and picture frames gleam like a silver shop. Even more calming is the view of the sad, wasted river, tawny as a lion, its back to the city (or is it the city that refuses to give its face to the river?). The Thames is too wide to flow, as the Seine does, through the heart of a city. The domesticated Seine, reciprocally reflecting the river's beauty and that of Paris. *Sous le Pont Mirabeau coule la Seine . . .*

She pulls back the curtains and watches the slow, tedious Thames with its escort of barges and tugs churning back and forth past warehouses and empty lots. Dickens, who loved his city so deeply, had good reason to fill his river with corpses that were first murdered and then robbed of valuables at midnight . . .

London turns its back to the river; she closes the curtains. She knows that the person knocking at the door of the apartment is Gabriel Atlan-Ferrara. Almost twenty years have gone by since she sang and he conducted *The Damnation of Faust* in Mexico City, and now there will be a repeat performance at Covent Garden, but just as when they were working together in the Bellas Artes they have wanted their first meeting to be private. The year 1949, and now the year 1967. She had been twenty-nine, he forty-two. Now she was forty-seven and he sixty, and both were a little like ghosts from their own pasts—or maybe it's only the body that ages, imprisoning youth forever within that impatient specter we call "soul."

Their prescribed meetings, however long it had been since they'd seen one another, were a homage not merely to their youth but to personal intimacy and artistic collaboration. She—and she wanted to believe that he as well—seriously believed that that was the gist of things.

Gabriel had changed very little, but at the same time he was more handsome. The gray hair, as long and unruly as ever, softened his slightly barbaric features, his mix of Mediterranean, Provençal, and Italian blood, with maybe a little Gypsy and North African thrown in (Atlan, Ferrara). The gray set off his dark skin and ennobled even more the broad brow while detracting not at all from the unexpected and savage strength of flaring nostrils or the perpetual grimace—for, even when he smiled, and today he was particularly happy, his smile was a bitter twist of wide, cruel lips. The deep lines in his cheeks and at the corners of his mouth he had always had, as if his duel with music left wounds that never healed. Nothing new. But when he took off the red muffler, a less preventable sign of age was visible beneath his chin; that skin had grown loose, even though—Inez smiled—since they shave every day men naturally slough off the reptilian scales we call "old age."

First they studied one another.

She had changed more than he, women do, more quickly, as if to compensate for their earlier sexual maturity—not just physical, but mental, intuitive. A woman knows more about life, and sooner, than a man, who is slow to give up his childhood. Perpetual adolescent or, worse, aged child. There are few immature women, but many children disguised as men.

Inez knew how to cultivate her identifying features. Nature had gifted her with a head of red hair that as she aged she could tint in the tones of her youth without attracting comment. She knew that nothing underscores the advance of years like changing hairstyles. Every time a woman changes her hairdo, she adds a couple of years. Inez let the flaming, naturally exuberant mane become her artifice: fiery hair was her trademark, contrasting with unexpectedly black eyes, not the green that usually goes with red hair. If age was gradually dimming those eyes, an opera singer knew how to make them gleam. The makeup that in another woman would be exaggerated, in Inez Prada the diva was an aftermath, or announcement, of a performance of Verdi, Bellini, Berlioz.

They stared at one another to reacquaint themselves and also to "run down the checklist," as Inez called it, using one of her many and frequent Mexican phrases, hand in hand, holding each other at arm's length, and exclaiming, You haven't changed, you're just the same, the years have been kind, your gray hair is so distinguished. They had had the good taste, in addition, to favor classic clothes: she a pale-blue peignoir, since a diva was permitted to receive at home wearing what she did in her dressing room; he a wool suit, black, but nonetheless showing the influence of the current street mode of *swinging London, 1967.* Both knew that they could never get away with dressing like kids, like so many ridiculous adults who didn't want to be left out of the "revolution" and suddenly forsook stodgy business attire and resurfaced sporting bushy sideburns (and advancing bald spots), Mao jackets, bell-bottom trousers, and macramé belts, or respectable matrons wearing four-inch Frankenstein platform shoes and miniskirts that revealed varicose veins not even pink pantyhose could disguise.

They stood like that for several seconds, holding hands, staring into each other's eyes.

What have you been doing all this time? How have you been? they asked each other with their eyes. They knew about the professional careers, both brilliant, both independent of each other. Now, like Einstein's parallel lines, they would finally meet at the juncture of the inevitable curve.

"Berlioz is bringing us together again." Gabriel Atlan-Ferrara smiled.

"Yes." Her smile was not so broad. "I hope it's not like a bullfight, a farewell performance."

"Or, as in Mexico, a prelude to another long separation. What have you been doing, what all has happened to you?"

She thought about it, and the first thing she said was, "What might have happened? Why didn't what might have happened happen?"

"Because it wouldn't have worked?" he ventured.

His body had recovered from the beating he received from the mustached man and his thugs in Alameda Park.

"But your soul hasn't . . ."

"I think you're right. I couldn't understand the violence of those men, even knowing one of them was your lover."

"Sit down, Gabriel. You don't have to keep standing there. Do you want tea?"

"No, thank you."

"That boy was nothing to me."

"I know that, Inez. I never imagined that you sent him to beat me up. I understood that his violence was directed against you because you'd thrown him out. I realized he was beating me so he didn't have to beat you. Maybe that was his idea of chivalry. And honor."

"Why did you leave me?"

"A better question, why didn't we make a move to get back together, either of us? I can also see it as your leaving me. Were we so proud that neither of us dared take the first step toward reconciliation?"

"Reconciliation," Inez murmured. "Maybe that wasn't it at all. Maybe that poor devil who beat you up didn't have anything to do with us, with our relationship."

It was a cold morning, but sunny, so they went out for a walk. A taxi took them to the church of St. Mary Abbots in Kensington, where as a girl, Inez told Gabriel, she had gone to pray. This church with the very tall steeple wasn't all that old, but it had an eleventh-century substructure that to her dazzled eyes seemed to surge from the depths of the earth and form the real church, as ancient as its foundation and as new as its construction. Everything conspired to make it all—the layout of the cloisters, the shadows, the arches, the labyrinths, and even the gardens of St. Mary Abbots—look as ancient as the abbey's foundation. It was, Gabriel commented, almost as if Catholic England were the self-confessed phantom of Protestant England, appearing like a mischievous spirit in the corridors, ruins, and cemeteries, all without images, of the Anglo-Saxon Puritan world.

"No images, but music, yes," Inez reminded him, smiling.

"Obviously as compensation," said Gabriel.

High Street is comfortable and civilized, lined with hardware and carry-out shops, stationery stores, office-supply shops selling typewriters and copying machines, children's boutiques, magazine-and-newspaper stalls, bookstores, and a large, open park behind an elegant iron fence: Holland Park, one of those green spaces that punctuate the city of London and give it its unique beauty. The main streets are utilitarian, wide, and ugly—unlike the *grands boulevards* of Paris—but they protect the secret of quiet little streets that with geometric regularity lead to fenced parks with groves of tall trees, manicured greensward, and benches where one can read, rest, or be alone. Inez loved to return to London and find those quiet oases where the only things that change are the seasons, and those unvarying gardens untouched by the tribal rites and noises with which youth announces its presence, as if silence might annihilate it.

Inez, wrapped in a long black cape lined with deerhide to offset the November cold, took Gabriel's arm. The conductor was dressed for the weather: wool suit and, wrapped around his neck, a red muffler that from time to time caught the wind like an enormous trailing flame.

"Reconciliation or fear?" Inez picked up the discussion.

"Should I have held on to you then, Inez?" he asked, not looking at her, head bowed, eyes on the tips of his shoes.

"Should I have held on to *you*?" Inez thrust her gloveless hand into Gabriel's jacket pocket.

"No," he observed. "I think that eighteen years ago neither of us wanted to take on the obligation of something that wasn't his own career—"

"Ambition," Inez interrupted. "Our ambition. Yours and mine. We didn't want to sacrifice that for someone else. Is it true? Is it enough? Was it enough?"

"Perhaps. I felt ridiculous after that beating. I never believed it was your doing, Inez, but I did think that if you were capable of going to bed with a character like that you weren't a woman I could love."

"Do you still think that?"

"I'm telling you I never believed it. It's simply that your idea of sexual freedom wasn't the same as mine."

"Do you think I went to bed with that boy because I thought he was inferior, someone I could toss aside on a whim?"

"No, I think it wasn't that you weren't discriminating enough, but actually that you were easily embarrassed, and that's why you made your choices public."

"So no one could accuse me of being a sexual snob?"

"No, not that either. Precisely so no one would think you discreet . . . That gave you even greater freedom. It had to end badly. Sexual relations have to be kept quiet."

Irritated, Inez jerked away from Gabriel. "We women are much better at keeping bedroom secrets than you men. You're all too macho, too much the peacock. You have to strut about like a triumphant kob after winning the battle over a female."

He stared at her pointedly. "That's what I mean. You chose a lover who *would* talk about you. That was your indiscretion."

"And that's why you left without a word?"

"No. I have a more serious reason." He laughed and squeezed her arm. "Inez, it's possible that you and I were not born to grow old together. I can't imagine you running down to the corner for a quart of milk while I shuffle out to look for the paper and we end the day watching the telly as a reward for being alive."

She didn't laugh. She disapproved of Gabriel's joke. He was straying from the real subject, which was about going separate ways after the *Faust* in the Bellas Artes. Almost twenty years . . .

"There's never a story that doesn't have its ghosts," Gabriel offered.

"Were there ghosts in your life all this time?" she asked with real affection.

"I don't know what to call the waiting."

"Waiting for what?"

"I don't know. Maybe for something that should have happened to make our being together inevitable."

"To make it fatal, you mean?"

"No, to avoid fatalism."

"What do you mean?"

"I don't really know. It's a feeling I recognize only now, seeing you after so much time has passed."

He told her he'd feared that love might bind her to a fate that wasn't hers and, maybe, selfishly, not his either.

"Did you have many women, Gabriel?" Inez replied in a mocking tone.

"Yes. But I don't remember a single one. What about you?"

Inez's smile turned to laughter. "I got married."

"I heard you did. To whom?"

"Do you remember that musician, or poet, or official censor, or whatever, who used to sit in on our rehearsals?"

"The fellow who loved the beans and tortillas?"

She laughed. Yes, that one: Licenciado Cosme Santos.

"Did he get fat?"

"He got fat. And do you know why I chose him? For the weakest and most obvious reason in the world. He made me feel secure. I have to admit he wasn't the he-man type who's a real stud, not the stallion whose sexual vigor never flags—and don't let anyone kid you, there's never been a woman who can resist that. But neither was he the great artist, the supreme ego who promised to be a creative partner only to abandon me, leave me all alone, in the name of the very thing that should have drawn us together, Gabriel: sensibility, love of music . . ."

"How long did your marriage to this Cosme Santos last?"

"Not even a minute." She made a little face, and shivered. "It wasn't a meeting of minds, or of sex. That's why we lasted five years. It didn't matter to me. But he didn't hold me back. As long as he didn't steal my thunder or meddle in my life, I tolerated him. When he decided to become important for my sake, poor man, I left him. And what about you?"

They had made a complete circle of the tree-lined streets around Holland Park and now were crossing a field where small children were playing soccer. Gabriel took his time answering. She felt that he was holding something back, something he couldn't say without affecting himself more than her.

"Do you remember when we met?" Inez said finally. "You were my protector. But then you walked out on me. In Dorset. You left me with a mutilated photograph from which a boy I would have liked to fall in love with had disappeared. Then, in Mexico City, you left me again. That's twice. I'm not berating you for it. You have the crystal seal I gave you on the beach in England in 1940. Do you think you can do me a favor now in return?"

"Possibly, Inez."

There was such doubt in his voice that Inez made hers warmer. "I want to understand. That's all. And don't tell me that it was the other way around, that I left you. Was it that I was too available, and you rebelled against something that seemed far too easy? You like to conquer, I know that. Did you think I was handing myself to you on a silver platter?"

"There's never been a woman as difficult to conquer as you," said Gabriel as they walked back to Kensington High Street.

"How do you mean?"

The sudden noise of traffic was deafening.

They crossed with the green light and stopped in front of the marquee of the Odeon cinema at the corner of Earls Court Road.

"Where do you want to go now?" he asked.

"Earls Court is very noisy. Let's go this way. There's a little alley around the corner."

They heard the loud soundtrack from the movie all the way down the alley, typical James Bond music. But at the end of the lane lay the small, shady, fenced-in park on Edwardes Square, with its elegant houses and iron balconies and flower-bedecked pub. They went in, found a seat, and ordered two beers.

Gabriel said, as he looked around, that a place like this was a refuge and what he felt in Mexico City was just the opposite. In Mexico there was no *shelter*, everything was unprotected, a person could be blotted out in an instant, without warning.

"And you abandoned me to it, knowing that?" Inez whistled, but not accusingly.

He looked her straight in the eye. "No. I saved you from something worse. There was something more dangerous than any threat of living in Mexico City."

Inez didn't dare ask. If he didn't understand that she couldn't ask him directly, she'd be better off saying nothing.

"I wish I could tell you what that danger was. The truth is, I don't know."

She wasn't angry. She didn't feel he was hiding anything when he told her that.

"All I know is that something in me prevented me from asking you to be with me forever. It was my loss and your gain."

"And you still don't know what it was that stood in the way, why you didn't tell me—?"

"I love you, Inez. I want you to be with me forever. Be my wife, Inez . . . That's what I should have said."

"Even now you won't say it? I would have accepted."

"No. Not even now."

"Why?"

"Because the thing I fear still hasn't happened."

"But you don't know what you're afraid of?"

"No."

"Aren't you afraid that what you fear has already happened, and that what happened, Gabriel, is what didn't happen?"

"No. I swear to you it hasn't happened yet."

"What hasn't?"

"The danger I am to you."

Much later, they wouldn't remember whether they had said some things face to face or only thought them as they looked at each other after all that time, or if they had thought them before or after their meeting, when they were alone. They didn't trust one another, didn't trust anyone. Who remembers exactly the order of a conversation, who knows exactly if the words in a memory were really said or only thought, imagined, spoken under the breath?

Whatever the case, before the concert Inez and Gabriel couldn't remember whether one of them had dared to say, We don't want to see each other anymore because we don't want to see each other grow old, and maybe for the same reason we can't love each other now.

"We're fading away like ghosts."

"We always were, Inez. I told you that there is never a story without its ghost, and sometimes we confuse something we can't see with our own unreality."

"Do you have any regrets? Are you sorry about something you could have done but let slip by? Should we have married in Mexico?"

"I don't know. All I can say is, it's our good fortune that we never had the dead weight of a failed love affair or an appalling marriage."

"Out of sight, out of mind."

"At times I've thought that falling in love with you again would be a sign of voluntary indecision."

"On the other hand, I sometimes think that we don't love each other because we don't want to watch ourselves growing old."

"But have you thought about how the ground would shake if one day I walked across your grave?"

"Or I across yours?" Inez hesitated, but laughed.

Atlan-Ferrara went out into the November cold thinking,

Our only salvation is to forget our sins, not pardon them but forget them.

She, meanwhile, stayed in the hotel and drew herself a luxurious bath, thinking, A failed love affair must immediately be put out of mind.

Why, then, did both Inez and Gabriel, independently, sense that this love, this *affaire*, wasn't over—however often they both might say not only that it had ended but maybe in the deepest sense that it had never begun? What was it between them that thwarted the continuation of what had been and prevented the occurrence of what never was?

Inez, soaping herself with pleasure, could have been thinking that the first throes of passion are never recaptured. Gabriel, walking along the Strand (German blitz in 1940, hippie bliss in 1967), would argue that ambition had outweighed passion, but the result was the same: We're fading away like ghosts. Both thought that at least nothing should interrupt the flow of events. And events now were not contingent on passion or ambition, or on the will of Gabriel Atlan-Ferrara or Inez Prada.

Both were exhausted. What had to be, would be. They would play out the last act of their relationship. Berlioz's *The Damnation of Faust.*

In her dressing room, dressed for the performance, Inez Prada was doing what she had been doing, obsessively, ever since Gabriel Atlan-Ferrara put the photograph in her hands and left the Savoy without a further word.

It was the old photo of Gabriel in his youth, smiling, hair tousled, his features less defined but his lips communicating a happiness Inez had never seen. He was bare-chested; the snapshot stopped at the waist.

Inez, alone in the hotel suite, slightly dazzled by the interplay between the silver decor and a winter sun pale as a child unborn, studied the photo, the stance of young Gabriel, whose left arm was held away from his body, as if embracing someone.

Now, in the dressing room in Covent Garden, the image was filling in. What that afternoon had been absence—Gabriel, alone, Gabriel, young—had gradually been changing; first the palest tints, then more and more precise outlines, and now an unmistakable silhouette, a palpable presence in the photograph. Gabriel's arm was around a slim blond youth who, like Gabriel, was smiling, a smile that was the precise opposite of Gabriel's, open, free of mystery. The mystery was the slow, nearly imperceptible materialization of the boy who had been missing from the photo.

It was a picture of a swaggering camaraderie, with the pride of two arrogant beings meeting and recognizing one another in their youth and swearing to stick together through a lifetime, never to be parted.

"Who is he?"

"My brother. My comrade. If you want me to talk about myself, you will have to hear about him."

Was that what Gabriel had said in the hotel? He had said it more than twenty-five years ago.

It was as if the invisible photo had been developed by Inez's obsessive gazing at it.

The photo she saw today was again the one she had seen during that visit to the cottage on the shore.

The youth who had disappeared in 1940 had reappeared in 1967.

It was he. No doubt.

Inez repeated the first words of their meeting: "Help me. Love me. *Eh-dé. Eh-mé.*"

She was overwhelmed with a terrible desire to weep over what had been lost to her. In her imagination she felt a mental barrier that sealed off the past: forbidden to touch memories, forbidden to step on already trodden ground. But she couldn't stop staring at that image in which the boy's features were filling in because of the intense gaze of a woman who was herself absent. Was it enough simply to concentrate on something to make the disappeared reappear? Is everything hidden merely awaiting our intense attention?

She was interrupted by her call.

They were midway through the oratorio, and she didn't come onstage, carrying a lamp, until Part Three. Faust has hidden. Mephistopheles has escaped. Marguerite is going to sing for the first time:

Ah, but the air is stifling!
I'm as frightened as a child!

Her eyes met those of Atlan-Ferrara, who was conducting with an absent, totally abstracted, professional air, except that his look denied that serenity, it held a cruelty and a terror that frightened her as she began the next line, *It was the dream I had last night that has upset me*, and, at that instant, though she was still singing, she no longer heard her own voice or the music of the orchestra, she stared at Gabriel as another song deep inside Inez, a ghost from Marguerite's aria, stepped outside her and into an unknown rite, took possession of her actions onstage as if in a secret ceremony that others, everyone who had bought tickets for the *Damnation of Faust* performance in Covent Garden, had no business watching: the rite was for her alone, but she didn't know how to enact it, she was confused, she couldn't hear herself, she saw nothing but the hypnotic eyes of Atlan-Ferrara recriminating her for her lack of professionalism—what was she singing? what was she saying?—my body doesn't exist, my body isn't in touch with the earth, the earth begins today, until she cried a cry outside of time, an anticipation of the infernal ride to the abyss that will end the opera.

Yes, blow, hurricanes,
Ring out, dark forests,
Crash down, boulders . . .

And then the voice of Inez Prada seemed to be transformed into first an echo of itself, then a companion to itself, and finally a different, separate voice, a voice with power like that of galloping black steeds, like beating nocturnal wings, like blinding storms, like the screams of the damned, a voice swelling from the rear of the auditorium and flowing toward the orchestra pit, first amid the laughter, then the astonishment, and finally the terror of the public: dignified men, clipped and powdered and shaved and handsomely attired, dried up and pale or red as tomatoes, and their women in décolletage and perfume, white as Brie or fresh as ethereal roses, the distinguished public of Covent Garden now on their feet, wondering for a moment whether this was the supreme audacity of the eccentric French conductor; was the "frog" Atlan-Ferrara capable of carrying to extremes this performance of a suspiciously "continental," not to say "diabolical," work?

The chorus cried out as if the oratorio had collapsed like an accordion, skipping all of Part Three to rush to Part Four, the scene of the violated heavens, raging storms, sovereign earthquakes, *Sancta Margarita, aaaaaaah!*

From the rear of the auditorium, advancing toward the stage, came a naked woman with writhing red hair, her black eyes glittering with hatred and vengeance, her mother-of-pearl skin scourged and bruised, carrying in her extended arms the motionless body of a little girl, a child the color of death, rigid in the arms of the woman, who was offering her as one would offer an insupportable sacrifice, a little girl streaming blood from between her legs, surrounded by the screams, the scandal, the indignation of the public, until this woman reached the stage, paralyzing the spectators with terror, presenting the body of the dead girl to the world as Atlan-Ferrara allowed the most ferocious fires of creation to flash through his eyes, his hands continuing to conduct, the chorus and the orchestra obeying, though maybe this was yet another innovation of the brilliant maestro, hadn't he said more than once that he would like to direct a naked *Faust*?; the exact double of Marguerite climbed naked to the stage with a bloody child in her arms as the chorus sang *Sancta Maria, ora pro nobis* and Mephistopheles could think of nothing to sing except the words of the lyrics but Atlan-Ferrara sang it for him, *hup! hup! hup!*, and the strange woman who had taken over the stage hissed *has! has! has!* and walked toward a motionless, serene Inez Prada, whose eyes were closed but whose arms were open to receive the bloody child and who, unresisting, let herself be stripped of her clothing, scratched, lacerated by the intruder with the red hair and black eyes, *has, has, has,* until both were naked, standing before a public paralyzed by conflicting emotions, the two of them identical except that now it was Inez who was holding the child, Inez Prada transformed into the ferocious woman, as in an optical illusion worthy of the grand mise-en-scène of Atlan-Ferrara the savage woman blended into Inez, disappeared into her, and then the one naked woman occupying the center of the stage fell to the floorboards still embracing the violated child, and the chorus exhaled a terrible scream,

Sancta Margarita, ora pro nobis
Has! irimuru karabrao! has! has! has!

In the stunned silence that followed the tumult only one ghostly sound is heard, notes never written by Berlioz, a flute playing a melody as swift as the flight of the raptor. Music of a sweetness and melancholy no one has ever heard before. A pale, blond youth the color of sand is playing. His features are so sculpted that one more stroke to his fine nose, his thin lips, or his smooth cheeks would have ruined, perhaps erased, them. The flute is ivory, it is primitive, ancient, or roughly made. It seems to have been recovered from the realm of oblivion, or death. Its solitary persistence wants to sound the last word. The blond young man does not seem to be playing the music. The blond young man is suffering the music; he occupies the center of an empty stage, facing a vacant auditorium.

It has been said. She will be again. She will return.

At that moment she will surrender herself to the only company that will console her for something that will begin to be sketched in her dreams as "something lost."

This her instinct will tell her. What is "lost" will be a timeless village that for her will forever be future, never *it was* but *now it will be*, because there she will live the happiness that was not lost, but will be found again.

How will it be, this thing that will be lost only to be found again?

It is what she will know best. If not the only thing, at least it will be the best thing she will know.

There will be a center in that place. Someone will occupy that center. It will be a woman like herself. She will see her and she will see herself, because she will have no other way to speak those terrible words *I am* without swiftly translating them into the image of the large figure sitting on the ground, covered with rags and metal, objects that will be deemed valuable enough to be traded for meat and vessels, for herds and precious staffs to be traded for other things—of lesser value, she will add, but more necessary for living.

There will be little she will want for. The mother will send men to look for food, and they will return, panting and bleeding, with boars and deer slung across their shoulders, but sometimes they will come back frightened, loping on four feet, and that will be when the father stands up and shows them, this way, standing, forget the other way, that is behind us, now we will be like this, on two feet, this is the law, and first they will stand up, but when the mother again settles her broad buttocks on the throne they will gather around her, they will embrace her and kiss her, they will pat her hands, and she will make signs with her fingers on the heads of her children, and she will repeat what she will always say, This is the law, you will all be my children, I will love all of you the same, none will be better than another, this will be the law, and they will weep and they will sing with joy and they will kiss the seated woman with great love, and she, the daughter, will join in the warm act of love, and the mother will repeat, ceaselessly, You are all equal, this will be the law, everything shared, whatever we need to live and be happy, love, protection, threat, courage, love again, all of you always . . .

Then the mother will ask her to sing, and she will wish that the protection she will always need will be forthcoming, that is what she sings.

She sings that she wants the company she will always long for.

She sings that she wants to avoid the dangers she will meet along the road.

Because from now on she will be alone and she will not know how to defend herself.

Before, we all had the same voice, and we sang without need to force ourselves.

Because she loved us all the same.

Now has come the time of a single chief who organizes punishments and rewards and tasks. This is the law.

Now has come the time to send away the women and to deliver them to other villages to avoid the horror of brother and sister fornicating together. This is the law.

Now has come a new time in which the father commands and indicates his preference for the oldest son. This is the law.

Before we were equal.

The same voices.

She will miss them.

She will begin to imitate what she hears in the world.

In order not to be alone.

She will be guided by the sound of a flute.

He conducted Berlioz's *Faust* for the last time in the Festspielhaus in Salzburg, the city to which he had retired to spend his last years. As he was conducting singers, chorus, and orchestra, approaching the apocalyptic end of the work, he wanted to believe that he was again the young maestro who had staged the work for the first time in a place he wanted, also for the first time, but one fatally pervaded with our past.

At ninety-three, Gabriel Atlan-Ferrara scornfully refused the stool they offered so he could conduct while sitting; he might be a little stooped, yes, but he would stand, because only standing could he invoke the musical response to a destructive nature that longed to return to the great beginning and there surrender to the arms of the devil. Was it true that, despite the clamor of the work, he was hearing footsteps approaching the podium, and then a voice in his ear: "Have you come to make amends?"

His answer was vigorous. He didn't think twice, he would die on his feet, like an oak, conducting the musicians, understanding to the end that music can be nothing more than an impressionist evocation and that it is incumbent on the conductor to impose the serene contemplation without which true passion cannot be instilled. That was the paradox of the music's creation. The old man had come to realize this, and that afternoon in Salzburg he wished he had known and communicated it in London in 1940, in Mexico in 1949, and again in London in 1967, when the idiotic public left the hall believing that his *Faust* was aping the nudist vogue of *Oh! Calcutta!*—never imagining the secret that had been exposed before everyone's eyes . . .

Only now, an old man, in Salzburg, 1999, did he understand the musical path from impression to contemplation to emotion. And he wished, with an inaudible moan, he had known that in time to tell Inez Prada . . .

How was the maestro going to tell the young mezzo-soprano singing Marguerite in Part Three of *The Damnation of Faust* that in his view beauty is the only proof of divine incarnation in the world? Had Inez known that? Conducting for the last time the work that had united them in life, Gabriel beseeched the memory of the woman he had loved:

"Be patient. Wait. They are looking for you. They will find you."

It wasn't the first time he had spoken those words to Inez Prada. Why hadn't he been able to say, "*I* am looking for you. *I* will find you"? Why was it always *others*, *they*, who were designated to look for her, to find her, *to see her again*? Never *he*.

The intense melancholy that Gabriel Atlan-Ferrara suffered as he conducted this music associated so closely with Inez's instinct resembled the act of touching a wall only to prove that it didn't exist. Can I ever believe in my senses again?

That last time, at the Savoy in London, they had asked one

another, What have you been doing all this time? so as not to ask, What happened to you? And certainly not, How will it end between us?

These isolated sentences meant nothing to anyone but him.

"At least we never had the dead weight of a failed love affair or an appalling marriage."

"Out of sight, out of mind, the English say."

Or, in Inez's Spanish, *"Ojos que no ven, corazón que no siente."*

The first passion is never recaptured. On the other hand, regret stays with us forever. Remorse. Lament. It turns to melancholy and lives in us like a frustrated ghost. We know how to silence death. We do not know how to quiet sorrow. We must be content with a love analogous to the one we remember in the smile of a face no longer there. But isn't that *some*thing?

I am dying but the universe goes on. I can't bear being separated from you. But if you are my soul and you live in me like a second body, my death will not be as inconsequential as a stranger's.

The performance was a triumph, a twilight homage, and Gabriel Atlan-Ferrara quickly and regretfully left the podium.

"Magnificent, maestro, bravo, *bravissimo*," the doorman said to him.

"You've turned into an old man I'd like to strangle," Atlan-Ferrara replied bitterly, talking to himself, not the aged and stupefied doorman.

He refused to allow anyone to walk him back to his house. He wasn't some disoriented tourist. He lived in Salzburg. He had already resolved that when he died he wanted to die on his feet, with no warning, no terror, no help from anyone. He dreamed of a sudden and loving death. He had no romantic illusions. He hadn't prepared any celebrated "last words," nor did he believe that death would afford him a lyrical reunion with Inez Prada. He had known ever since that last night in London that she had left with someone else. The blond youth—my comrade, my brother—had disappeared forever from his youthful photograph. He was . . . elsewhere.

"Il est ailleurs." Gabriel smiled, satisfied in spite of everything.

But Inez was "elsewhere" as well. She hadn't been seen since that November night in 1967 at Covent Garden. Since the public believed that what happened was part of Gabriel Atlan-Ferrara's imaginative *mise-en-scène*, any explanation was acceptable. The media reported that Inez Prada had disappeared in a puff of smoke through a trap door in the stage, with the child in her arms. Pure effect. *Coup de théâtre.*

"Inez Prada has permanently retired from the stage. This was the last work she planned to sing. No, it wasn't announced, because then attention would have been directed to her farewell performance and not to the Berlioz itself. She was a professional. She always put herself second to the work, the composer, the conductor, and, as a result, the venerable public. Yes, a complete professional. She had an instinct for the stage."

Only Gabriel was left, his hair black and unruly, his dark skin burned by sun and sea, his smile brilliant . . . Alone.

He counted his steps from the theater to the house. It was a mania of his old age, counting the number of steps he took every day. This was the comic part. The sad part was that with every step he felt the wounded earth beneath the soles of his feet. He imagined the scars that were accumulating on the always deeper and harder layers of the crust of dust we live on.

Ulrike, *die Dicke*, was waiting for him with her hair rebraided and her apron starchy crisp and her gait painful, legs wide apart. She set a cup of chocolate before him.

"Ah!" Atlan-Ferrara sighed, dropping into his easy chair. "Passion is gone. We are left with hot chocolate."

"Be comfortable," his servant told him. "Don't worry. Everything is in order."

She looked at the crystal seal occupying its usual place: the tripod on the little table in front of the window framing the panorama of Salzburg.

"Yes, Dicke, everything is in order. You don't need to break any more crystal seals."

"But, sir, I—" his housekeeper sputtered.

"Look, Ulrike," said Gabriel, with an elegant wave of the hand. "Today I conducted *Faust* for the last time. Marguerite has ascended to heaven. Forever. I am no longer the prisoner of Inez Prada, my dear Ulrike."

"Sir, it was not my intention . . . Believe me, I am a grateful woman. I know I owe you everything."

"Easy, easy. You know perfectly well you don't have any rivals. I need a servant more than a lover."

"I'll fix you a cup of tea."

"What's the matter with you? I'm already drinking my chocolate."

"Sorry. I'm very nervous. I will bring you your mineral water."

Atlan-Ferrara took the crystal seal from the stand and rubbed it.

He spoke in a quiet voice to Inez.

"Help me stop thinking in the past, my love. If we live for the past, we elevate it to the point where it usurps our lives. Tell me that my present is to live attended by a servant."

"Do you remember our last conversation?" Inez's voice answered. "Why don't you tell the whole story?"

"Because the second story is a different life. You live it. I'm holding on to this one."

"Is there anyone whose existence you're denying?"

"Maybe."

"Do you know the price for that?"

"I'll take it away from you."

"So? I already lived it."

"Look at me carefully. I'm a selfish old man."

"That isn't true. You've spent all these years looking after my daughter. I'm grateful for that, I thank you from the bottom of my heart."

"Bah. You're being sentimental. I treat her as who she is."

"But I thank you anyway, Gabriel."

"I have lived for my art, not for easy emotions. Goodbye, Inez. Go back to wherever you are." And he put back the seal.

He looked out on the landscape of Salzburg. Imperceptibly, it was beginning to dawn. He was surprised at how quickly the night had passed. How long had he been talking with Inez? Only a few minutes . . .

"Didn't I always say that the next performance of *Faust* is always the first? Take notice, Inez, of my resignation. The next reincarnation of the work will not be in my hands."

"There are bodies born to wander and others to be made flesh," Inez told him. "Don't be impatient."

"I'm not, I am satisfied. I was patient. I waited a long time, but in the end I was rewarded. Everything that had to return, returned. Everything that had to be reunited, was. Now I must be silent, Inez, so I don't break the continuity of things. Tonight in the Festspielhaus I felt you near me, but it was only a feeling. I know you are very far away. And as for me, am I something more than a reappearance, Inez? Sometimes I ask myself how people recognize me, how they know to greet me, when obviously I am not who I am. Do you still remember who I was? Wherever you may be, do you hold a memory of the person who sacrificed everything so that you could *be* again?"

Ulrike was standing looking at him, not hiding her scorn.

"You're talking to yourself again. That's a sign of senile dementia," said his housekeeper.

Atlan-Ferrara heard the unbearable sounds of the woman's movements, her stiff skirts, her key ring, her feet dragging from her painful walk, the parted legs.

"So is there another seal, Ulrike?"

"No, sir," said the housekeeper, her head lowered as she picked up his cup and saucer. "This one here in the living room is the last—"

"I'd like it again, please."

Ulrike held the object in her hands and showed it to the maestro, her expression brazen and arrogant. "You know nothing, maestro."

"Nothing? About Inez?"

"Did you ever see her when she was truly young? Did you really watch her grow old? Or did you simply imagine it because calendar time said it was so? How was it that you grew old between the fall of France and the blitz and the time you traveled to Mexico and came back to London while she stayed the same? You imagined her growing old to make her as old as you."

"No, Dicke, you're mistaken. I wanted to make her my eternal, my one thought. That's all."

Dicke laughed long and loud, and thrust her face close to her employer's, ferocious as a panther. "She won't be back now. You are going to die. Maybe you will find her somewhere. She never abandoned her own land. She came here for only a brief time.

She had to go back to his arms. And he will never come back. Resign yourself, Gabriel."

"All right, Dicke," the maestro sighed.

But to himself he said, Life passes so swiftly, a haven whose only purpose is to offer death a place to exist. We are the pretext for death's life. Death gives presence to everything we have forgotten about life.

He walked with slow steps to his bedroom and carefully examined two objects on his night table.

One, the ivory flute.

The other, a framed photograph of Inez, gowned forever in the costume of *Faust*'s Marguerite, her arm around a barechested, towheaded young man. Both were smiling openly, without mystery. Never to be separated.

He picked up the flute, turned out the light, and with great tenderness played a passage from *Faust*.

The servant heard him from far away. He was an eccentric, mad old man. She loosened her braids. Her long white hair fell to her waist. She sat on the bed and held out her arms, muttering in a strange tongue, as if convoking a birth or a death.

The memory of the lost land will not console her.

She will walk along the shore and then turn away from the sea.

She will try to remember how her life was before, when she had a companion, a hearth, village, mother, father, family.

Now she will walk alone, with her eyes closed, trying in this way to forget and to remember at the same time, shutting out sight in order to surrender to pure sound, trying to be what she can hear, only that, longing for the murmur of the stream, the whisper of the trees, the chattering of monkeys, the roar of the storm, the galloping of aurochs, the clash of the antlered beasts over a female, everything that saves her from the solitude that will threaten her with the loss of communication and memory.

She would like to hear a cry of action, unconscious and interrupted, a cry of passion tied to sorrow or happiness, she would like especially for the two languages, that of action and that of passion, to blend together so that the cries of nature would again be converted into desire to be with the other, to say something to the other, to shout her need for and sympathy for and attention to the other, lost to her since she was driven from her home, expelled by the law of the father.

Now who will see you, who will pay attention to you, who will understand your anguished call, the call that will finally be torn from your throat as you run uphill, beckoned by the height of the stone cliff, closing your eyes to relieve the duration and the pain of the climb?

A cry will stop you.

You will open your eyes and you will see that you are at the edge of a precipice with empty space at your feet, a deep ravine, and, on the other side, on an outcropping of stone, you will see a figure who will shout to you, who will wave his arms, who will say with every movement of his body but most of all with the strength of his voice, *Stop, don't fall, danger . . .*

He will be naked, as naked as you.

The nakedness will identify you, and he will be the color of sand, all over, skin, body hair, the hair on his head.

The pale man will call to you, *Stop, danger.*

You will understand the sounds *eh-dé, eh-mé, help, love,* swiftly being transformed into something that only in that moment, as you shout to the man on the other shore, you will recognize in yourself: he is looking at me, I am looking at him, I am shouting to him, he is shouting to me, and if there were no one there where he is, I would not have shouted the way I did, I would have shouted to frighten away a flock of black birds or from fear of a beast crouching nearby, but now I am shouting to ask something or to thank this other person, who is like me but different from me, now I am shouting not out of necessity but desire, *eh-dé, eh-mé, help me, love me . . .*

He will come down from the rock with a pleading gesture that you will imitate with cries, unable to avoid reverting to grunting and howling, but both feeling in the swift trembling of your bodies that you will run to hasten the meeting so desired now by you both, you will revert to the earlier cries and gestures until you meet and embrace.

Now, exhausted, you will sleep together in the streambed at the bottom of the precipice.

Between your breasts will hang the crystal seal that he will have given you before he makes love to you.

That will be the good part, but you will also have done something terrible, something forbidden.

You will have given another moment to the moment you are living and to the moments you are going to live; you have perverted time; you have opened a forbidden field to what happened to you before.

But now there is no warning, there are no fears.

Now there is the fullness of love in the instant.

Now whatever may happen in the future must await, patient and respectful, the next hour of the reunited lovers.

CARTAGENA, COLOMBIA, JANUARY 2000